Formal Affairs

Formal Affairs

Jeanne McCurley

PALMETTO
PUBLISHING
Charleston, SC
www.PalmettoPublishing.com

© 2024 Jeanne McCurley
All rights reserved.
No portion of this book may be reproduced,
stored in a retrieval system, or transmitted in
any form by any means—electronic, mechanical,
photocopy, recording, or other—except for
brief quotations in printed reviews,
without prior permission of the author.

Hardcover ISBN: 9798822960954
Paperback ISBN: 9798822960961

To Brennan for taking this walk with me hand in hand.

Table of Contents

Prologue 1
Chapter 1 3
Chapter 2 21
Chapter 3 32
Chapter 4 49
Chapter 5 64
Chapter 6 79
Chapter 7 87
Chapter 8 95
Chapter 9 105
Chapter 10 117
Chapter 11 124
Chapter 12 134
Chapter 13 142
Chapter 14 152
Chapter 15 157

Prologue

A wise woman once told me, "Perform your wifely duties, and everything else will work itself out."

It wasn't until now that I know two things: First, that was a very old-fashioned, conservative view of the matrimonial obligation of a "good girl." Second, that was total bullshit! Hmm...not so wise after all.

Unapologetically every single day forces decision-making, an uncertain gamble leading to a series of choices and resulting consequences. Simultaneously appearances may serve to complicate matters when what the eyes see as factual, based on appearances, is merely a snap judgment of immediate emotional reaction. Such is the case with matters of the heart, especially mine.

I'm not a newcomer to contemplating the varied views and expectations of matrimonial obligations, never quite determining the "right way" to be a wife or husband. Surely gender roles evolve over time, right? Thoughts ping-pong in my unsettled mind, seeking answers I'm never relieved to discover. I contemplate the weight parents' views should carry on the matter when they're born in a totally different generation. Surely generational gaps exist when deviation from existing societal norms fails to occur across decades. Believe me, a mother's words ingrained in a developing and eventually maturing mind over time bears the enormity of influence!

Mother had neither interest nor tolerance for marital complaints, no matter how big the issue, because to her, if your husband isn't happy, it's your fault. You're either a poor manager of money, a lousy housekeeper, or a frigid plaything. "Keep your husband happy and he won't stray" was her mantra. If a husband looks the other way, it's because you aren't satisfying him. In that case the immediate, superficial solution would be to buy something sexy, add another coat of mascara and a spritz of perfume, and throw yourself at him, regardless of his interest or lack thereof. In Mary Ann Newman's mind, a wife's sole purpose on earth is to ensure the total happiness of her husband by any means necessary. No matter what, no questions asked, not debatable. Regardless of the answer to the question, "Does mother know best?" here I am. Once again I consider the span of suggested acrobatic antics and question the depths one must travel to entertain a partner, committed or otherwise, if only for appearance's sake.

Chapter 1

My best friend from childhood, Misty, and I savagely scoff down a plate of savory meatballs and spaghetti, fully loaded with garlic, during a quick lunch; evidently, carbs are not a major factor today. We are an hour away on a business appointment and must return to work soon, yet once again we find time to contemplate virginity's significance on the wedding night. "Virginity…to be or not to be? You know my position on the matter, and I'm not talking doggy-style, ma'am. Mommy dearest made sure *her* beliefs are *my* beliefs."

Misty lets out an exasperating sigh and comments so loud half the patrons of a quaint little lunch spot—Mia's Italian Eatery—can hear. "Ha! Any self-respecting young maiden from the Deep South would never consider allowing a man to mount her from behind, my friend. And to penetrate that sacred territory with a hot beef injection… unheard of. Missionary all the way! Seriously, Kristen, you know that load of crap was forced down our naïve, lusty throats and drilled into our innocent, formative little virgin minds from the time we could walk. But here we are now, decades later, still giving that bullshit narrative the time and attention it definitely does not deserve! I have to say, though, *your* mother takes the cake on the bullshit meter." Misty's assessment of Mary Ann Newman was dead on.

Attentive patrons tune in and chuckle at my response. "No shit, she's a pro!" In my best southern drawl impersonation of Mom, I add, "Ladies and gentlemen, I am 1967 Miss Alabama Peach, y'all, and it's been such an honor and privilege to pose for you in my alpine white, one-piece halter-top swimsuit, just like the one Marilyn Monroe used to wear. Feel free to take my photo and, gentlemen, I'd be happy to grace your bedroom walls as a pinup poster!" Mom was a complete flirt but situationally played innocent. It was not a privilege to have my formative years molded by a fake old-fashioned prude with double standards who secretly, especially after peeking at her father's porn collection on a leisurely Sunday afternoon, yearned to make the acquaintance of a handsome gentleman's bulge.

Mother, an eternal "belle of the ball," earned multiple beauty pageant titles all along the Gulf Coast region—Strawberry Festival Queen, Ponchatoula, Louisiana; Miss Biloxi Beach Babe, Biloxi, Mississippi; and Voodoo Queen, New Orleans, Louisiana. A stunningly beautiful young woman with thick black hair and large, dark expressive eyes, her touch-me-not vibe, small waist, and swaying hips had men swooning for her attention. She flirted and teased mercilessly, batting those eyelashes like hummingbirds' wings. That is, all before finally settling down in her midtwenties with John Newman and flaunting her wedding ring as a trophy. Mary Ann's personality—Type B, strongly conservative yet outspoken only in close women's circles—believes that only sluts or paid whores partake in "the naughty" before marriage. Mary Ann and her snooty socialite clique still share views of their touch-me-not predecessors dating back to the days of horse and carriage, where complete submissiveness was owed to your "husband," and I use the term "husband" loosely, as their male counterparts rarely bought into the *shared* level of commitment theory. Poor Mary Ann, always putting on the charm, never daring to leave home without a full face of makeup, teased-up tresses, and pushup bra—a total Stepford Wife stereotype—still expects to be seen as a southern beauty queen. Her most prized possession, most valued title is her name, Mrs. John Newman.

"Misty, I need one of our weekend binges and really soon." Historically, when either of us feels overwhelmed and headed for a crisis, we take off to the beach and check into a hotel before spending countless hours with endless bottles of wine, taking in the swooshing of countless ocean waves, and simply talking it out to a solution. November in the South is an especially favorite time to go to the beach, as the temperatures finally mellow, complete with cool breezes and low humidity. Now is the time.

"I don't want to get too deep into it on our lunch break, but I'm getting some uncomfortable vibes from James that aren't sitting right, like female intuition making my 'alert, alert, your marriage may be in trouble' radar activate. Maybe it's nothing, maybe it's paranoia, maybe it's just raging hormones with the impending arrival of 'Uncle Red' coming to town any day now, but I'm feeling like the effort is turning one-sided. Like especially in the last few months, I've been the only one putting forth any effort. I can't quite put my finger on it, but my instincts are telling me that James is distracted, his mind elsewhere. I know his job keeps him super busy, especially since he's taking on more of a leadership role in his family's business, but I feel that he's different, secretive maybe. Naturally, or at least automatically, my mind turns to infidelity. Maybe just paranoia? Maybe not. I don't want to be one of those women claiming, 'I had no idea!'"

Misty knows me way better than anyone else in the world. I really need her logical way of looking at things and her no-bullshit attitude to tell me if she gets the vibes my marriage is on the brink or not. Relying on her keen instincts has never led me astray. Plus she's known James for as long as I have; I'd consider her nearly an expert on our relationship since she's been with me through the good and bad, my sole confidant.

Misty and I are closer than sisters, inseparable for longer than memory serves. Our mothers realized they grew up only blocks away from each other while in conversation. Chatting in the waiting room at the pediatrician's office, it was decided Misty and I would be registered for art lessons at age three. From there, we took piano lessons and ballet lessons and had weekly playdates while the moms gossiped incessantly and sipped spiked lemonade. Two generations of gals were becoming fast friends.

All the big *firsts* were experienced together, best friends from Jump Street. We cautiously shaved our legs for the first time in middle school together and waxed the dreaded pubes from our bikini area on my bathroom floor before getting totally shit-faced, jungle-juice daiquiris the culprit, during ninth grade year in our tight bikini bods. We confided in each other the things that "good girls" just didn't publicize. Those magical first kisses and tingling sensations when a pair of sixteen-year-old good-looking

7

baseball players literally "rounded the bases" of our previously untouched bodies, stopping short of home base anyway. Donna Summer's "Bad Girls" became our summer anthem. We cried together over first-time broken hearts and the shame worn as a surrendered battle flag when the feeling of being used and discarded was too deep to handle alone. We bonded over the loss of innocence in the early days and accumulated secrets and mistakes later. Sorrow took center stage when Misty's father became ill and passed away during our 10th-grade year, leaving her mother a financially unstable, alcohol-addicted widow. Lost in grief, Misty's sorrow and depression almost took her life as her intolerable, relentless grief overcame her. Sadly, unable to ease the pain, she sought relief by cutting herself, hiding the infliction beneath long-sleeved shirts. But her scars were more than physical afflictions; her hurt was apparent in her sad eyes, solemn moods, and apparent lack of hope. She refused to open up to anyone but me, and I had no idea how to help except to simply *be there* for her. Luckily Misty emerged from the darkness, adapting to living with the gaping hole in her heart left by her father's far too soon departure.

In turn she supported me when an obsession with my weight consumed me almost to the point of anorexia, always trying to stay slim and "keep the eye" of the gentlemen, just as Mary Ann said, did, and encouraged me to do. Excessive amounts of exercise combined with minimal caloric intake allowed me to drop the pounds quickly. Misty thought it wasn't a good idea, saying she read that losing weight too quickly would most assuredly make it come back faster when I started to eat normally again.

Looking back it was all experimental—responses to sadness, excitement for our collective *firsts*, doing anything for attention, and finding solutions when our screwed-up decisions packed the potential to ruin our reputations or, worse yet, our futures. We made it through countless trials, but we understood the true meaning of friendship and still do.

However, regarding my extreme weight-loss venture, it was a comment from James that really hit home and snapped me into better judgment. Watching me walk across the school cafeteria and grabbing a seat next to him, with nothing but an apple in hand, he asked, "Are you sick or something?"

In sharp response, I replied, "Not at all, why would you ask something like that?"

"You just seem to have lost a lot of weight in so little time. You're starting to look too skinny, almost scarecrow-like." Clearly irritated, and facial expression displaying disbelief at his insensitivity because everyone knows what a touchy subject body image plays for teenaged girls, I shot back, "Don't guys prefer thin over fat?"

"Not when it makes you look sickly. Healthy is sexy as fuck. You looked beautiful just the way you were. Stop trying to go rail thin." And that's all it took to end my weight-loss obsession. James had noticed me in a physical way.

Misty was there when I married James not very long after high school because "good girls get married and began families," according to Mom anyway. And James's family pedigree was quite nice, which suited Mary Ann's standards, enabling her to brag to her snooty friends whose daughters' hands had been passed over by eligible, financially secure gentlemen.

"What's the big hurry?" Misty asked when we were sharing a dorm in year one of college life. "I mean, we all know you and James are going to get married, but it still seems like rushing. Can't you both agree to finish college first? Is your mom really pushing you that hard? She's probably scared you're going to ditch him for a laborer of some sort, *heaven forbid!*"

"You don't understand; *pressures* are rising," I tell her as I slowly drag the word, "and the tension between James and me is escalating. It's getting harder to hold him off."

"What the hell, girl, can you just fuck the man already? This is ridiculous. Instead of enjoying that gorgeous being who, by the way, appears to be packing much more than the *Average Joe*, you're still worrying about holding up that 'good girl' facade? For fear that *Mommy* might get mad?" she asked in a sarcastically whining tone. With that, my mind replayed Mary Ann's nagging but deliberate comments.

"This is a family we want to join with. They are good upstanding people in the community. You won't want for anything. Plus, James is easy on the eyes; you won't mind so much performing your wifely duties. You might even learn to like it. And believe me, if you don't snag that handsome man, there will be a line of girls desperate to capitalize on your ignorance."

Mother insisted I fight the good fight playing hard to get, as she deemed herself the prototype of Miss Prim and Proper. Despite the inner conflict I fought against her ploys of manipulation to protect appearances for judgment's sake, I simply could not help myself from becoming the "descendant of purity" she wished her audiences to see. Truly I was in love with James almost immediately.

At the young age of seventeen, beginning our junior year of high school, James Montgomery caught my eye in a mesmerizing way. A solidly built, ever-so-handsome guy with dark-blond hair and piercing greenish-gray eyes, James was the object of many girls' desires. He wasn't the captain of the football team, or any sports team for that matter. He wasn't one of the "bad boys," sporting long, untamed hair and smoking under the stadium, making girls degrade themselves to be noticed and eventually be invited into the back seat of their cars. Rather, James was a clean-cut, sexy-as-sexy-can-be, confident alpha male who was definitely going places after high school, and all the girls were well aware. Because his last name was Montgomery, and mine was Newman, I was, more often than not, assigned to sit in the desk behind him in alphabetical order. This boy was different, exuding an air of maturity and purpose. His confidence rang out daily as he responded intelligently to questions in class, hyperfocused on success, internalizing that effort in high school would prepare him for his next step afterward. Misty and I watched many girls flirt mercilessly with him, all but lifting their miniskirts to gain his attention, and I know he enjoyed the chase. After all, he was still a young man with testosterone running through his veins. Despite a teenage male "testing the waters," James had no intention of allowing "loose" girls to entrap him in a relationship or otherwise. James and I were friends first, and although he was simply gorgeous, I never let on that I found him absolutely striking. He clearly became comfortable talking with me about anything, and we did for hours on end. James confessed that he had always been attracted to me but even more so because I didn't chase after boys or turn into a slut like many of our classmates did. We became inseparable, each other's sounding board for sanity's sake, unable to not communicate for more than a few hours. For that reason, James and I developed an intense friendship that eventually blossomed into love and ultimately marriage.

While James and I dated, it wasn't easy holding him off physically. Knowing he could initiate his sexy gaze and have any girl begging him for sexual relief, I had to keep him temporarily satisfied by allowing a fair amount of kissing and touching. I told him all the usual claims of *good girls* like, "It's so important to me to save myself for marriage," and "It will mean so much to us both for my first time to be on our wedding night," and "James, you know I'm a faithful, God-fearing woman; it's a sin before marriage," and "It won't be as special if our first time is on any random date." For the most part, James respected my decision, although there were times when we fought—fought to keep our hands off each other and fought because I wouldn't give in. The heavy "petting," another of Mother's antiquated terms, was my only salvation. Plus I feared if Mary Ann saw me after, she would know immediately that I had been *deflowered*.

I can recall James's pleas: "Come on, Kristen, you've got to give me something here, more than a hug and a peck. We've been dating for long enough; you shouldn't keep torturing me like this. I'm in love with you, and I'm craving the feel of you. I know you feel how intense our connection is. It can only grow deeper if we let this happen." His sincere desire to be as close to me as two people can be played with my mind—guilt, guilt, guilt. He wasn't the only one with desire. I know he masturbated often because he wasn't getting relief from me, and that tore me apart too.

Then other times he would give ultimatums out of sexual frustration. "You must not love me the same way I love you," or "Is there somebody else that you're holding out for?" Then a fight would start. Different circumstances, same outcome…no intercourse. James even approached the subject of oral sex as an alternative, and I nearly came unglued! That was a subject we had never talked about before, assuming it would just eventually happen once we got the first fuck out of the way. Scared, I turned the conversation to my advantage by describing how much pressure he was putting on me when I was simply not ready. I reminded him of how it was my practicing of abstinence that he also respected me for. That argument landed in my favor for only a short time, until he then took the position, "This is what monogamous couples do."

"Holy shit! If he's asking about blow jobs and kissing privates, we need to get you ready," Misty exclaimed. "Lickie, lickie—a woman's alternative to dickie dickie! But not for the faint of heart!"

I let out a huge sigh, complete with an animated eye roll. I was most definitely not ready to go *there* yet.

"I'm so glad you find this funny, Precious. This is my life here, dammit. It's so easy to make light of the situation when you're not the butt of the joke, and it's not *your* relationship on the line." Feeling my desperation, my best friend did what any best friend would do—partnered up with me to raid my dad's porn collection. Talk about a fast-tracked education. Taught, but not *prepared*. All mechanics and no emotions.

My own fears sometimes got the best of me—worried that he would finally tire of the no-sex game and break up with me for somebody who would give herself freely and often to him. Or maybe he would cheat on me to get off instead. Either way it was a huge burden to carry, a race against time, a balancing act that neither of us was winning. With James and I following different plans of study at the university, we didn't have any of the same classes. In fact, we rarely saw each other during the day, and because of work and studying, we saw less and less of each other in the evenings. The insecurities started taking a toll on me as I worried that some other free-spirited college girl would catch his attention. Even with James's constant reassurance that he was in love with me, arguments were frequent as I became increasingly jealous and controlling over time. I knew I held the power of liberation in my hands. I had a big decision to make. And so it was, to end the charade, we decided on a wedding date.

Young girls dream of their perfect wedding, and I did plenty of that. But for me it was also a mind game turned anxiety-ridden event. Having been brainwashed that virginity is something to be saved for the wedding night, the anticipation of the unknown was overwhelming. I was taught that sexual pleasure is for the man, and it's almost a reward a man gets when he officially gives a woman his last name as if it's a special gift reserved for a select few. "If you're one of the lucky ones, you'll find a good husband. If you're especially lucky, he'll be good-looking with a great job. You, Kristen, can have it all." Of course Mary Ann was implying it won't be any of those skanky whores who provide free, no-strings-attached pussy at bachelor parties so future husbands can prevent embarrassment and report they "have experience." "You must play the game well and make him fall in love and want you for longer than a *quickie*," she added. "We Montgomery women do not allow ourselves to be used and discarded."

"You know I have your back. Best friends forever, remember?" Misty says, "But, shit, we have to leave now, or we won't make it back for two o'clock." Misty's right; we have a ten-member bridal party, not including the mothers and grandmothers of the bride and groom, coming in for a private appointment. Both sides of the intended family made it clear that money was free flowing, and they expected royal treatment. We had grown accustomed to the "type"—those with the snooty air about themselves, those who demanded high quality and exceptional personal service, and those who would avoid at all costs outfitting their bridal party with department store fashion. Pretentious and demanding as these customers may be, their patronage contributed to almost instant success for Formal Affairs, and we appreciated them for it, catering to their every wish. Misty and I humbled ourselves to avoid "killing our cash cow."

A fashion major in college, Misty supported herself by working in a small vintage boutique while I took paid internships with a variety of businesses to gain experience, not sure what I wanted to do post college. One weekend, Misty and I, quite tipsy on cabernet, decided we should go into business together. Given my business and marketing degrees combined and her retail experience as well as our shared obsession with weddings and formal attire, we decided to become partners in Formal Affairs, the swankiest bridal boutique in South Louisiana. Initially, people tried to discourage the partnership, claiming that it would ruin our friendship; however, five years into the venture has proven to be beneficial to us both. Shortly after opening our business, plans for expansion proved to be the logical next step. Our vision included becoming almost a one-stop wedding-attire shop. Formal Affairs was initially located in one store in a strip mall, but with our first year's profits, we managed to purchase a lovely, large stand-alone Victorian-style house that we gutted and remodeled, designating separate areas for evening gowns, bridesmaids' dresses, wedding gowns, and tuxedo rentals. There was another separate space dedicated to shoes, undergarments, and accessories. A final benefit of frugal spending was private offices for Misty and me, an unexpected but gratifying perk. We painted the exterior of the house bright white, planted lush landscaping around the perimeter, positioned a stone path leading to the massive brick entryway, and hired an interior designer to decorate in rich shades of ivory and gold. There were plush couches and fancy chairs, soft, velvety curtains with tasseled tiebacks concealing fitting rooms, crystal chandeliers, and stagelike, carpeted platforms made for admiring oneself before the vast mirrored walls. We served champagne to full bridal parties as they bonded together, giggling and scrutinizing the countless gowns their brides-to-be modeled in search of *the one*. *Southern Dreams* magazine described Formal Affairs as "extremely classy and charming, seeping with southern hospitality." Contrary to early, repeated skepticism, Misty and I were successful in business, and our bonds of friendship only strengthened.

"Misty, is it a midlife crisis? I've always loved James, but have I always known what love really is?" James Ethan Montgomery claims the title of my first love, thief of my attention, taker of my virginity—NOT before the wedding night, of course—and holder of my heart for the greater part of my thirty-eight-year life.

I've also been told that there are seasons of life, and one season will begin and eventually end to make way for another. Has my season of being in love with James headed toward its demise, or has his being in love with me run its course? Is that what's happening in my marriage? We've grown so distant, and I know something just isn't right anymore. I start wondering where and when it all went wrong, and I can't even remember when it felt right. Or maybe it was never good, and I was just too young to know anything different. Maybe it's all my experience with bullshit meters. I can't make heads or tails of it.

"Do you still want James? I mean, *really* want James?" Misty's question is sincere and thought-provoking. Taking a minute to consider the magnitude of the question, I toss my head back taking in the ceiling tiles, then glare at numerous paintings of Italian villas gracing the painted stucco walls. With authentic Italian melodies softly sounding in the background, I deliberate before responding.

Leaning in, my voice is a low whisper as I state, "Define *want*." Blurred lines and mottled thoughts appear. How do you know if you want someone? I have more questions than answers. Do I want him to be happy? Sure. Do I want him to come home to me every night? Again, sure. Do I want him to make an effort to act like a committed husband? That would be nice. Do I want him to touch me in ways that draw goose bumps and make me feel alive?

Fucking right! One lingering question remains, though… does he *want* me?

"What the fucking hell?" Misty's jaw drops, her stunning lined hazel eyes pop wide open, and she tries to divert my attention from the window. Her sleek ponytail sharply snaps back and forth from my oblivious face to the window. She repeats as if stuttering, "Oh my God, oh my God, oh my God." Bending to peer around her enables me to catch the scene, turning her face and neck a bright shade of crimson. I can't speak. Frozen with no muscle movement. Paralysis taking hold. I just got my answer.

Chapter 2

"What the actual fuck?!" Misty yells as we take in the sight of James in a full-on embrace with a woman I don't recognize. The hug lingers for an extended time—at least five seconds. Staring across the street at them, I watch as my husband pulls back and goes back in for a kiss on the cheek while Miss Long Red Hair and even longer legs throws her head back, willingly accepting the affection of this sexy hunk of man before her. In clear public view, she returns the kiss, smiles a sultry "fuck me right here, right now" expression, and flings her thick, glossy hair over her right shoulder, engaging him in easy, apparently playful chatter. I'm mesmerized by her classy, sexy seasonal outfit, a style only worn during a short two- to three-month window outside of Louisiana's usual heat and humidity. The camel-colored suede miniskirt with a formfitting silk animal-print blouse cut low enough to show excessive cleavage is quite enough. However, paired with the thigh-high, *bend me over the table and take me from behind* stiletto boots send me mentally over the edge. I can feel my face getting flushed. What is my husband doing with this woman? An hour away from his office? On a random Tuesday? Is he *seeing* her?

Stunned, I watch the interaction. They're not strangers to each other. There's a familiarity and comfort between them as James places his hand on the small of her back and leads her into a local specialty shop, Coffee & Cocktails, where customers are welcomed beneath a purple canopy. He leads her inside to *our* favorite table, acting like it's the most natural movement in the world.

James and I shared so many intimate conversations there, indulging in our favorites—red wine for me, Crown and Coke for him, and music for us both. The place is a personal favorite of ours, the location of our official first date, the place where James and I crossed the line, making the transformation from friendship to legitimate couple. And I'm on the receiving end of instant heartbreak. It was here that James and I nurtured our love of music and built our repertoire of favorites by genre. We sat for hours at a time analyzing lyrics to any and every song played, applying meaning to our personal beliefs and experiences. We had no favorites, claiming every genre had its place and was a great fit situationally. For each occasion certain music fits best. At a wedding one would expect to hear some love songs mixed with classic party music and line-dancing tunes. At a barbecue country rock would be a good fit. Before a ball game, tailgating music would be expected. For an easy Sunday sipping wine, old-school R & B or light rock would complement the day. Outside washing the car, rock and roll would add inspiration to the task, and so on. Whatever the event music would always complete it. Our connection grew, and we found commonality through our musical passion.

Peering through the window amid the flow of traffic, I watch with my heart in my throat.

"Go over there!" Misty furiously grabs my attention back to our table. "What are you going to do, sit here and watch that bitch with your husband?"

I still can't move. It's like people and interactions are flowing in slow motion around me. Misty starts beating on the table. "What the hell are you doing? Get over there right now! Why aren't you doing anything?" Misty's frantic expression jolts me from my trance.

Unable to form a sentence, a lone tear trails down my drained face. Pain-stricken but coherent, I stutter on my words as shock and unfathomable hurt turn into an immediate call to action. I grab my cell phone from my purse and quickly shoot off a text to James.

Me: Hey, just checking in. How's your day going?

From across the street, I see James look down at his phone before putting it into his pocket. Extremely pissed, I say, "Oh hell no, motherfucker, you are NOT about to dismiss my text while you are laughing and carrying on with some redheaded bimbo!"

Me: Did you have lunch yet?

James reaches down to retrieve his phone, looking irritated. He silences it again. I dial his number. It rings… and rings…and rings. Apparently he put it in silent mode because the relentless ringing is neither phasing the *happy couple* nor the patrons at the neighboring tables. Growing angrier by the second, I dial several more times, hanging up when a voice responds, "The mailbox is full." Continuing to watch this shit show, I see the woman rise, apparently excusing herself to visit the restroom, as a text comes across my screen.

James: Sorry, I missed your calls. I'm in an important meeting. Is everything OK?

Misty grabs my phone and starts to type back, "Are you fucking around on my best friend, you asshole?" I snatch the phone; she reaches to grab it back. Struggling and gaining ultimate control, I'm in possession of the phone, and before she can send the message, I'm frantically deleting her angry words. Unbelievably my rational side takes over. I know I need to process what I'm seeing rather than react out of emotions.

"Just go back to the boutique. I need to wait this out." How long has this been going on? What actually is going on? Apparently they didn't just meet, so who is this woman, and why is my husband ignoring me? It hurts to watch, I feel a vomit coming on, but I'm stilled by the playful banter they exchange with ease.

"Are you crazy? I'm not leaving you here in a state of shock. I'll call Sunny and ask her to reschedule the bridal party appointment. This is a crisis! Would you leave me by myself to deal if I just found out my husband is cheating on me with a hot redhead? I think *not*. Or at least it better be NOT!"

"We can't do that, Misty; they're about to drop a fortune. Remember, this is the group that wants only to view the most prestigious, high-dollar designer labels. We can't afford to miss out on these orders. This is *my* problem to handle. Please just go. I'll meet you there in a little while; I've got to see how this plays out." I am not about to leave this scene without knowing how it ends. I'm actually hoping that what I'm bearing witness to is not what my gut is telling me. "Besides, we can't do that to Sunny. She's the only other person at the shop right now who can manage the fittings. She'll need help locating the correct sample sizes, pinning the gowns, finding the proper undergarments, and handling the estrogen overload!"

I remember clearly the day Sunny walked into Formal Affairs. She had a spunky character like I'd never seen before. With tiny stature but bold, jet-black spiked hair boasting purple tips, she was a jolt of personality. "Who owns this place? I'm looking for a job," she said, quickly absorbing her unfamiliar surroundings and making eye contact with me.

I told her I did, but she would have to make an appointment to talk.

"I worked down the street at the department store, but I finally reached my limit and quit. That hateful hag of a boss lives to bitch at me. She says I don't have to punch a damn time clock, but she watches me like a hawk! She's dreadful!"

"Look," I breathe out in exasperation, "like I said, you'll have to make an appointment. Can't you see the place is jam-packed with high school teenagers searching for the perfect prom dress?"

Without hesitation, Sunny jumped into action, hauling gowns into fitting rooms for growingly impatient patrons. From that point on, Sunny joined our staff and extended family two years ago, and her bubbly personality, in addition to her endless stories of casual promiscuity, keeps us entertained for hours on end. Sunny represented the free sexual spirit we wished we had the nerve to be aside from our dirty dreams. Sunny called things as she saw them—very bold and abrasive. Conservative she was not. Once Sunny said, "Your husband is absolutely gorgeous, and he treats you like his queen; if I didn't love you like a sister, I'd be in line to fuck his brains out. Twice on Sundays!" We laughed hysterically.

Truth be told, secretly I wondered if she would ever act on that if she had caught James's eye. That sort of comment is just not something to say out loud. Hell, what's the difference between simply *thinking* it as opposed to *speaking* it? Hadn't I, at times, thought about how hot someone else's husband was or how attractive some of the men were who came to the boutique to get fitted for tuxedos? Dismissing Sunny's comment as innocent, I wholeheartedly felt I never had a reason to think James wasn't 100 percent devoted to me and our marriage.

"You know I don't want to leave you like this, but I see the point. I'll only go if you promise me you're in a safe headspace and that you won't do anything crazy—without me anyway." Emotionally torn, Misty slams her hand on the table hard enough for the remaining half-eaten meatball to hop into her lap. "Shit!" she yells. Flinging the meatball off, cursing under her breath, she turns to make a quick exit out the back door, not wanting James to see her from Coffee & Cocktails's window across the street.

Stinging like a motherfucker, I see the waitress deliver James a cocktail. No doubt a Crown and Coke. His flirty "friend" appears to be laughing hysterically at something he says and giving him deep fuck-me eyes. Her right leg, crossed over the left, bounces freely while she apparently keeps beat to the rhythm that must be playing in the background. I know all too well the atmosphere over there, especially the music selection James and I spent hours enjoying once upon a time. I see her exposed thighs, too, because that damn miniskirt barely covers her coochy! I struggle to read their lips, but I can't; their profiles won't allow it. But any logical person can tell that they are way too *into* each other's vibe.

Defeat and helplessness take over, and I do what any self-respecting wife would do…I pick up the phone and call his office. "Hello, Montgomery Insurance Agency," a voice greets me on the other end. It's Rose, James's secretary. Rose and her husband, Henry, are dear family friends of James's parents, and she came to work with the agency just to help out when they first opened. With their children grown and Henry not ready to retire, Rose became a permanent fixture.

"Hi, Rose," I say in as calm a voice as I can muster. "Can I speak with James, please?"

"I'm sorry, Kristen, but James isn't available right now. If you'd like, I can ask him to give you a call back when his meeting is over."

"Did you say he's in a meeting, not at lunch or anything?"

"Oh no, he's in a meeting here at the office and asked not to be disturbed." With the other lines ringing in the background, Rose hurries me off the phone to catch the other calls. She wishes me a good day.

So now he's got Rose covering for him? This shit can NOT be happening! Why would Rose take part in lying to me? I never imagined her to be that way, but then again she's a friend of my in-laws first and foremost. She's always thought James to be the cat's meow, the total package, and I've always had an eerie sense she thought I was holding James back from marrying an heiress or someone holding any sort of prestigious title. Rose truly thought James to be deserving of his heart's desire. From where I sit at this moment, his fucking black heart is desiring something it shouldn't be. I clearly see where her loyalties lie.

Mystery woman bends over, showing an excessive amount of boobage for my taste, although apparently not for my husband's as her hand emerges from her designer bag with what appears to be an iPad. *What is she doing with that thing?* Clearly firing it up and motioning with a head nod for James to come and sit next to her, he eagerly moves his chair beside hers, smiling his million-dollar smile. *Damn, is there even six inches between their chairs?* Mystery woman is in control, swiping, typing, flirtatious smiles, and I haven't seen James this attentive in forever. He's deeply immersed in whatever she's showing him. Could they be planning some sort of getaway? Am I making assumptions? Jumping to conclusions? I think not. Why wouldn't he take her to our favorite all-inclusive resort in the Bahamas? I mean, he had mystery woman meet him at our place after all. He's keeping this meeting a secret from me, refusing to answer my calls and texts, lying about his location, engaging in physical contact—hugs, touches, kisses, sitting too close—having his secretary cover for him, meeting an hour away from the office, I'm sure for secrecy's sake, thinking I'll never find out. *Well, surprise, surprise, motherfucker! I'm here, and I see you! You are not about to make a damn fool out of me.*

My phone buzzes. "What's happening?" Misty's text flashes across the screen. "It's been like ten minutes, and I haven't heard from you yet. Is he still with that woman? I need play-by-play."

I dial her number, she answers immediately, and I respond, "Yeah. It looks like she's writing something down on a piece of paper, maybe a business card. It's too far away to tell. He's reaching over, takes the card, and studies it before tucking it into his jacket pocket." He reaches out his hands for hers, their gaze never leaving the other's face. Silence ensues.

"Kristen? Kristen? Talk to me. What's going on?"

"I'm about to come unglued, staring as my life passing me by." Swiping my phone to access the camera, I take several snapshots. The continuous camera click records in slow motion my husband walking this woman to her waiting car, designer sunglasses now covering those sultry eyes. An intimate, lingering embrace follows. I've seen enough.

Chapter 3

For now it takes every ounce of my strength to head back to the boutique. Sitting in the back of an Uber for an hour's drive allows me processing time to sort my short list of immediate priorities. First and immediately, I must push this mess aside until the bridal party's order is secured, complete with a deposit, because the profit margin is huge, way too good to pass by. Misty and I can treat ourselves *and* our employees to a well-deserved, hefty bonus. Second, I'm going to keep this shit to myself, aside from Misty, who just bore witness to my husband's advertised lack of commitment to me, until I can get away to clear my head. I can't let my humiliation and emotions give my knowledge away too soon. James can't know about what I saw, not yet, not until I decide what to do about it. Next I have to keep from throwing up. *Damn, I really need to throw up!*

Finally I'll revise my hotel reservation at the Beau Rivage Casino scheduled for Saturday, moving it up to a Thursday arrival instead. The weekend bridal bizarre being held at the Gulf Coast Coliseum provides the perfect escape since I'm already attending as a store owner. This will give me a few days alone, away from the humiliating shit show that has become my life. I desperately need to get away from here sooner rather than later. Oh, and let's not forget that one nagging thought flittering in and out during this drama—Mary Ann's accusatory voice condemning me for not being a good wife to James. Why do I let her have this effect on me?

My phone starts ringing in my purse. James's name lights up on my screen. And so it begins. *Fake it till you make it, Kristen.* Except I can't. I can't do it. I can't bring myself to physically talk to this manipulative asshole. Not yet. The emotions are too raw; the sting is still fresh. I let the call go to voicemail. Playing it back, I hear, "Hey, baby, I just finished up with my first meeting and thought I would give you a call before heading into my next one in about ten minutes. I guess you're busy, so I'll just see you at the house tonight."

Another damn lie. Apparently James has become quite the seasoned liar, with deceit flowing naturally from his forked tongue. He doesn't stumble, nor does he exhibit an ounce of remorse. *Does he seriously take me for a fool?*

Does he think I'm that naïve and my trust in him is infinite to the point that I just accept anything he says? Does he believe I will just fall for anything and take his word without question? My, my, James, how quickly you've become the skilled serpent. Trust is the basis of a healthy marriage, an important piece to build with your partner, and it should not be taken for granted. His actions have gone far enough without accountability, and I've simply and innocently encouraged it.

The closer we get to Formal Affairs, the faster my heart beats and the anxiety intensifies. Again the feeling of nausea grips my insides. The Uber drops me off in a fairly packed parking lot, which means the store is full of patrons shopping for their upcoming happy occasions. It also means that I may be able to fly under the radar, avoiding the studying eyes of the employees and Misty. I'm in no position to carry on light conversations or even to answer prying questions.

Sunny is the first to spot my entrance. "Hey, boss, I'm so glad you made it back. There are a ton of messages for you behind the counter. Ms. Morrison called to schedule a fitting appointment, and she'll only talk to *you*." Sunny exaggerates an eye roll. "The Anderson party wants to know if they qualify for a discount if they order more than seven dresses from last season's line. Oh, and a man named Drew called. He didn't leave his last name but asked specifically for you. He said he would call back later. And…shit, I can't remember the rest. Like I said, the damn messages are behind the counter."

"Sunny, seriously, do I have to constantly remind you to watch your language when we have customers?"

Sunny rolls her eyes for the second time in two minutes. "Whatever, it's not like these uppity rich people have never heard or used a curse word before. Besides, my va-jay-jay needs some tending to, so excuse me, boss, while I try to find a sexy stud to handle me, if you know what I mean?" She gives me a wink before turning to haul a stack of newly delivered boxes by Chad, our hot FedEx guy nicknamed Dreamy Chad, containing black, patent leather shoes toward the tuxedo room where a group of guys stand ready for their fittings. They seem to be a rowdy bunch, laughing and fist-bumping and sharing a flask of a dark-brown liquid, I presume, more ready for tailgating than trying on bow ties and tails.

I call out to Sunny, "Did Drew say if he was calling about a personal event or if he was a vendor?" With the big bridal show happening this weekend on the Gulf Coast, I have several calls in to the business office because I haven't received tickets that were supposed to be emailed. "Hopefully, he's calling to explain why I still don't have the entry tickets, although the credit card was charged."

She shrugs her shoulders and crudely pumps her hips as if air humping, responding, "Didn't say if he was an event organizer," while balancing the mountain of boxes.

Help me, Jesus. This girl is about to pimp herself out and drag down our reputation while she gets her rocks off! Or maybe I should join her myself. My "rocks" could certainly be tended to as well.

It's back to reality when Misty sneaks up on me. "How are you making out? Never mind, I can see the answer for myself. You're about to bust out crying. Don't give him the satisfaction. Why don't you cut out early? We can handle things here. Besides, Dreamy Chad's delivery today was small, only the men's shoes we ordered, so there's no unpacking, sorting, and tagging to do. Inventory entry is already done." Just then, I receive a text.

James: Don't forget, we're having dinner at my parents' house, so I'll just meet you there. I almost forgot except my mother just called to let me know that Rose and Henry will be coming too.

Isn't this cute? Let's not disappoint Mommy. Instead, let's just lie to the wife I'm supposed to be committed to.

Kristen: I'm really not in the mood to have dinner with your parents. Make an excuse for me.

James: Not going to happen. We canceled on them last week.

So smug! You, asshole, are in no position to dish out directives!

Kristen: I'll probably have to work late. The store is packed.

Hold that thought. Actually this might just be the break I need. I won't be alone with James. Rose, who is now my sworn enemy for covering my husband's lies, will talk for hours on end. Nosy Rosie is a fitting nickname for her. She's always asking about my customers, their sizes, and how much they paid for their clothing before making the details part of her gossip ring—Rose knows. Bless poor Henry for putting up with such an old biddy bitch! No wonder Henry doesn't want to retire; she's what he has to look forward to! This evening, however, Rose's prying nature, her pursuit to gain inside, private information with the intent to spread forth to the masses, will be used to my advantage.

Kristen: I'll get there as soon as I can.

"I'm OK, Misty. James just reminded me of dinner at my in-laws' tonight. We'll get home late, and I'll probably start packing. I'm changing my hotel reservation to arrive on Thursday afternoon. This works out perfectly. If he questions me about anything, I'll tell him I'm just distracted, trying to get everything done, including payroll, before attending the show. I'll learn to master a lie as easily as he does. Tomorrow and Thursday I'll come into the office early, before James leaves for work, so we can get all the orders submitted, set the fitting appointments, complete payroll, and review the show's designers and agenda. Then I'll head to the Gulf Coast after lunch Thursday. We can keep your room booked for Saturday."

"You don't want to share a room with me?" she asks.

"It's not that. I just really need some alone time to get lost in my thoughts. We'll still have meals together and drinks after the show on Saturday and Sunday nights. If I end up crying all night, I don't want to keep you awake. It's just better this way."

"OK, I'll let you slide this once because I know what a prick James is. Also Thursday is too early for me to get there because I don't have a sitter for Chloe. Mom and Dad will be on a cruise, and my sister isn't available until Friday at the earliest."

Precious little Chloe, Misty and Mike's six-year-old daughter, is a big part of our life. We've committed to being the best godparents a child could ask for. Having kids of our own is something we put on the back burner for now. Earlier in our marriage, James's priority was building his client base, and mine was on fashionably dressing the men and women of the Greater New Orleans area for their important occasions. Besides, James knew from the beginning that I was adamant about not starting a family until we could move out of the house his parents bought for us. Although my biological clock is ticking, and the window of motherhood is slowly narrowing, I can't muster the thought of staying in our current home for the rest of my life. My mother-in-law wants to play hardball, controlling her son by moving him around the corner, OK, she won that round. But I'm not about to give her anything else she wants, especially a grandchild, until I get out from under her claws, disguised as a house…the perfectly extravagant wedding gift. James claims the house was free. That couldn't be further from the truth. It comes with a hefty price tag of indebtedness.

Picking up on the conversation disrupting our own, right there in front of us, Sunny is handing her cell phone number to what I'm hoping is an eligible bachelor, meaning no strings attached, like wife and/or children. If not, it wouldn't be the first time. That girl seriously is a horndog on the loose! Head shaking left to right, shoulders rolled back to a perfect posture, keys in hand, I head toward my first public act of deception—dinner at the Montgomerys'.

So maybe dinner at the in-laws is not the best idea. As I pull up to the expansive, almost-obnoxious-in-size, Acadian-style home, I see the joyful interactions in the dining-room window like the outsider I claim to be tonight, and I start sweating. *What are you thinking, Kristen? This could be a disaster. You want to scratch James's eyeballs out!* Through the window I see him conversing effortlessly with his father and Henry, a confident, handsome smile gracing his face, and it pisses me off to no end. *How can he socialize so nonchalantly, appearing to have not a care in the world? His lies and indiscretions have ruined our marriage, and he's apparently the life of the party. Misty's right…James IS a fucking prick!*

I need a minute or so to "fix my face," Misty's term for setting a fixed appearance, becoming almost stoic, not flaunting emotions. Glaring at the home brings me temporarily back to the conversation James and I had prior to our wedding when he first told me of his parents' *surprise* wedding gift.

Surprised, I asked, "For real, your parents are buying us a house?"

"Not buying, they already bought. You're really going to like it. It's right off the main street in town, on one of the few streets that still had picket fences, conveniently located to all your favorites…a coffee shop, a bookstore, several restaurants, a gym…the list goes on and on. And it's the perfect size for us, not too big or too small." He was trying to convince me this was an innocent and selfless act of giving. There went the bullshit meter, quickly ascending.

"Wait, you knew about this and have actually seen it?" I was suddenly feeling deliberately left out. "What if I don't want to live there? We talked about renting an apartment for a few years until you break away to start an independent insurance agency, having gained enough of your own clients, and I could build my and Misty's business to a solid point and start saving money. I don't like the fact that your mother gets to determine where we live, and of course it's in the same neighborhood she lives in! Can't you see she's trying to keep her hold on you?"

James became irritated, and he had no problem showing it. "Are you seriously pissed off that my parents are buying us a house? So many people never get to own a home. You're coming off as an ungrateful brat. What do you want me to do, tell my parents thanks, but no thanks? We'd rather rent an apartment for years rather than accepting your generous gift?"

My responses came out in a pleading, desperate tone. "James, you know as well as I do that we are going to be stuck there for much longer than we planned because, after all, how long is long enough to appreciate the damn wedding gift without hurting their feelings? I would rather tell your parents that they shouldn't have done this without our consideration and that we intend to purchase a home in the suburbs like we talked about!" Then I tried to make him see that he was going back on the decisions we made together. "You promised me I could have the home I've always dreamed of, a traditional redbrick with white columns, outdoor kitchen, swimming pool, large kitchen, and…something that *I* picked out, not your controlling mother!"

"Look, Kristen," he said, "I want those things, too, but can't we have them both? The house would give us a great start. It is paid for. We won't have to pay rent. We can save even faster and then build the house we truly want."

Seeing that I was not going to win that argument, I delivered my final attempt at making my position known. "Ugh! I'll go along with this only if your parents are told they should not make decisions for us and that we are thankful for the gift but intend on buying in the suburbs once we're financially secure. For the record, I don't even want a damn picket fence!"

Unsurprisingly, James never spoke a word about it to his parents, except for his extreme gratitude. And so it was, once again, mothers controlling situations with authoritative influence, leading us into doing things *their* way under the guise of maternal generosity.

My face is fixed, literally and figuratively, as I enter the home of Barbara and Edward Montgomery. "Oh hello, Kristen dear. So happy you could fit us into your schedule this time." Of course Barbara starts our interaction in her traditional manner, with snide, passive-aggressive comments. She typically makes it known that *she* is the only person who puts my husband first.

I shoot right back at her, "Well, you know how it is, Barbara, the working women of today no longer resemble their counterparts of yesteryear who couldn't manage both a career *and* a personal life. I'm happy I could join you as well." *Take that, bitch!* The smirk on my face is fierce competition for hers. This woman does *not* want to challenge me tonight of all nights. I may be easily inclined to tell her to go fuck herself.

James approaches me, landing a kiss on my cheek as I feel my body go rigid. "What's the matter?" he asks, while nudging me off to the side of the room.

"What's always the matter, James? Your bitch of a mother started her crap as soon as I walked through the door. I've had enough of her. Just so you know, if she continues with the underhanded comments, I won't be held responsible for my comebacks. I told you this dinner was not a good idea."

As he nods in his *let's keep the peace* gesture, I leave him there, heading to my next victim…Rose. These people have no idea of the venom I can strike with tonight if provoked.

Feeling the buzz of the phone in my pocket, my eyes capture Misty's name on the screen.

Misty: How's it going? Are you keeping it together over there?

Kristen: It's together, all right, but not bitch-slapping my damn mother-in-law, a wolf in sheep's clothing, will be a huge triumph. She deceptively poses as a concerned, loving mother, but I can spot a control freak a mile away! Hell, I don't know; between that underhanded impostor, her conniving son, and his manipulative secretary, I should just get the hell out of here before I do something I'll regret.

Misty: Hang on, friend. Prison orange is not your color. Once you get past tomorrow, you'll get the quiet time you need. I think going to Biloxi early is just what the doctor ordered.

Kristen: Add some alcohol to that prescription.

Misty: You've got this! Love you.

Kristen: Thanks for the encouragement. It's helping. Love you too.

Deliberately taking the seat across from Rose enables me to have to speak loud enough for all to hear. "So, Rose, guess who came into the store this week? Celeste Chapman and her daughter, Monica. They're in the beginning stages of planning her wedding and wanted to get some pricing information before bringing the whole bridal party in."

Rose lifts her head, a malicious grin on her face. "That's because Celeste is going to have to take out a second mortgage on her house to afford the expensive taste that spoiled-rotten daughter of hers has. She's never been able to tell her no, and the ungrateful monster she created knows just how to control her mother." Barbara and Rose break out in laughter. Rose adds sarcastically, "I'm sure she'll have to spread the charges among her many credit cards."

Barbara contributes, "You know, unappreciative children should really practice good manners by expressing thankfulness for the generosity of others. They don't *de-*

serve the gifts they are given. They should appreciate their parents' love and acts of kindness."

Here we go again, comment number two and I've only been here fifteen minutes.

"Unless those acts of kindness are executed with ill-intent, you know, for selfish or controlling reasons," I retort. The glare in Barbara's eyes could burn a hole right through me; that is, if I let her close enough to do it. She may be classified as family by marriage, but I know without a doubt she is an enemy by trade.

Rose fights for my attention. "So, Kristen, tell me about the Wellingtons. How much is dear Pamela paying for her daughter's gown? I overheard her chattering in the beauty salon, claiming that it was well over ten thousand dollars. Is that true?" Here's my chance to strike revenge on Rose for hiding James's lies, as she and Pamela have a long-standing relationship built on nothing but jealousy. Jealousy aimed toward Pamela for her impeccable lineage, her gorgeous home, which welcomes tourists during the holiday season to gawk over her beautifully decorated estate, and her natural ownership of high societal class that Rose could never exhibit always strikes a nerve.

"You should see the gown; it's absolutely stunning! Yes, it comes with a hefty price tag. Pamela wasn't exaggerating. Don't quote me, but just thinking of the designer she went with, we are talking anywhere between a range of ten to twenty-five thousand dollars. It is completely embellished with crystal beading. And that doesn't even include the veil. In fact, I am visiting a bead distributor this weekend before I attend the bridal bizarre in Biloxi. There's a specialty shop that accommodates store owners by appointment only, and I managed to get one. Apparently the Wellingtons want to match the beading patterns on the cathedral-length veil too. They are truly spending a fortune." *Lies, lies, lies…take that, you bunch of hypocrites!*

James asks, "When is the appointment? I thought you weren't leaving until Saturday morning?"

"It's actually Thursday evening. I called in a favor, asking for a private appointment since many of the designers we carry adorn their gowns with specialty beads and crystals. So I had to revise my travel plans. I'll be heading that way after lunch Thursday." James looks displeased.

***

At home a few hours later, I've already washed off my makeup, determined to keep busy by the time James walks through the front door. I can hear him storming toward the bedroom. His face…oh, that perfect face I've loved for so many years…that face with the lying set of lips attached to it immediately starts hammering out the questions. "When were you going to tell *me*, your husband, about your little trip? I don't appreciate being blindsided in front of everyone!"

"You already knew about the bridal bizarre this weekend, and the bead appointment just came up today. I didn't have the time until then to fill you in. I mean, I don't always know what *you're* doing? In fact, I texted you several times today *and* called, but you didn't even answer. I'm not seeing a problem," I state calmly but sarcastically.

"Look, you know I get busy at work and have a lot of meetings during the day. I did try to call you back when I was available. I just would appreciate knowing what my wife is doing before anyone else does."

"You know, James, maybe you should try to get out of the office some during the day instead of holding meeting after meeting. You could make yourself more *available*. It might improve our communication and do wonders for your tan."

"What is that supposed to mean, Kristen?" He barks at me. "We *both* have high-demand jobs."

"Just what I said. You're always in the office. Maybe sunlight would improve your mood and help you to see things objectively, like the fact that we don't communicate as much as we should. Possibly because you're always too busy."

"OK, I'll give you that. It's been weeks since I've been able to get out of the office."

James, you are such a fucking liar! If only I could confront him. Not now. Slowly heading toward the shower, he begins unbuttoning his shirt, manly chest hair and masculine chest in plain sight. He knows I've always had a thing for a man in a white dress shirt, but this motherfucker is not about to try to get me to have sex with him! *Don't look, Kristen; don't look, Kristen. He's going to lure you in with that sex appeal, girl, don't do it. Gather your pride and take it with you!*

Turning to walk out of the bedroom, I call back to him from over my shoulder, "I've got some emails to catch up on; don't wait up for me." Actions speak louder than words.

Always someone who appreciates solitude and silence, I refrain from putting on the television. Natural background noise is what I enjoy most—the humming of the ceiling fan, the low rumble of the refrigerator, the chirping of insects outside, and the occasional car passing by. A different noise in the distance captures my attention. It's the voice of James on the phone in the bedroom. Behind the closed door, he thinks I can't hear him, but I can. Tiptoeing closer I make out his words: "It was great to see you too. When can we meet again?" There's a silent pause. For a second I fear he feels the proximity of my presence. Then I realize he most definitely does not. "We have to be careful. Do you think anyone saw us today? Let's pick somewhere different next time. My wife is acting kind of suspicious tonight." Another pause. "This has to be *our* secret. She can't find out."

Chapter 4

I have it made. Or do I? Shouldn't every middle-aged man reflect on his accomplishments when he is approaching forty years of age? I rock back and forth in my oversized office chair. My large office, which hasn't always been this size, is richly decorated in dark leather, sleek, modern fixtures, and one-of-a-kind works of art, souvenirs Kristen and I picked up during our travels over the years. The insurance agency has grown from its humble beginnings basically consisting of my father, Edward, with one secretary, my mother, Barbara, into a major company employing more than fifty people, including a combination of agents and clerical staff. Gradually my father acquired more and more clients because of his good business sense and providing excellent customer service. Edward Montgomery emerged from a small business owner taking out a loan to chase his dream, to that of building a regional insurance empire. Not only has my father become a successful entrepreneur, envied by his competition, but also his character and financial status deem him an esteemed community member, serving in leadership positions on various business councils.

My professional business cards boast of my title and accomplishments. I'm outfitted in an expensively tailored three-piece suit and designer shoes. Modeling picture-perfect style, I'm always dressed to impress. My name is embossed on my leather portfolio, which I carry into meetings, and my engraved gold pen, an anniversary gift from Kristen, is attached for convenience. I drive to work and to visit clients in a black Mercedes S-Class sedan, the status of accomplishment. I notice the flirtatious manner in which females interact with me. This has been the case for most of my life, but I've never taken advantage of it once Kristen and I got married. I've heard coworkers, whose whispers are anything but that, privately complimenting my looks, and I'm sure I could get a quick blow job from any one of them…but intermingling business with pleasure is not my thing. Exploring those invitations would not be a smart move; I've worked too hard to build my reputation to endanger it with a quick fuck. I live by the saying instilled in me by my father: "Don't shit where you eat." Great advice as it is, I'm not completely convinced Dad has applied it himself. Either way, my parents' marriage is not my concern. It's hard enough to keep my own on track, trying to balance my and Kristen's work schedules while having a social life too.

We've been lucky to have our "go-to" couple, Misty and Mike, always on standby and quite flexible, even though they are a couple with a kid. Little Chloe is such a sweet little girl, so she sometimes gets to tag along. Maybe I've been selfish, but having children hasn't been a priority—partially because Kristen and I have been hyperfocused on our careers, building financial and professional security, and also because I never wanted to share her attention. We have always had the freedom to do what we want, whenever we want, which has included extensive travel. And we deserve that lifestyle for making sacrifices along the way. Our life together seems to be enough for both of us as it is. We don't feel like we are missing anything. I guess now, with Kristen's indifference and the growing distance between us, things happen as they are intended to.

To the general public, I appear to have it all together. The truth is, however, I'm far from the picture of perfection I'm portrayed to be. Oddly, though, I strove for perfection for the greater part of my life, seemingly always within reach, only to fall short. I'm not a perfect son, not a perfect boss, not a perfect friend, and certainly not a perfect husband. The business is booming, and I'm finally making a six-figure salary, but professional success and steady money aren't enough when something is missing in my personal life. Maybe for far too long I took for granted that Kristen would always look at me the way she used to. Something shifted between us along the way. Not only are we drifting apart, but she's also started to make excuses to be away from me and not include me in her plans the way she always had. For instance, why didn't she tell me about going to the Gulf Coast earlier? She certainly could have sent a simple text.

Phone buzzing, I see Mike is calling.

Mike: Hey, man, what's up? You free to catch a game Saturday? Since the girls are going to that bridal thing, I thought we could pick a sports bar and have a few drinks.

James: Yeah, I'm free, but why don't we meet up with Kristen and Misty in Biloxi first, maybe Friday night, and watch the game there on Saturday? They already have reservations.

Mike: No, Misty isn't going until Saturday morning.
James: Oh, I forgot.

No, I did not forget. My lovely wife failed to mention that she was going alone. *What is going on with her? Why didn't she tell me Misty isn't meeting up with her until Saturday?* I look like a fool right now, not knowing what my wife is doing.

James: Look, I have to run. Text me the time LSU is playing, and I'll swing by and pick you up Saturday before the game.

Rose's voice comes over the intercom. "James, your mother-in-law is on hold for you."

"My phone didn't ring, why did it come to the reception desk?"

"Silly James, Mary Ann called for *me* first. She heard a radio advertisement about the bridal bizarre this weekend and wants to try to get a group of ladies to go. I told her I didn't think it was open to the public, but she said she would try to get tickets through Kristen's business."

"OK, put her through." It takes another minute before my phone rings. I guess the two old biddies are yacking it up. "Good morning, Mary Ann, what can I do for you?"

"Hello, James dear, I was wondering if you could talk to Kristen about getting myself and a few others from my book club into the bridal bizarre this weekend. I tried to call her, but she's not answering her phone."

That's probably because Kristen's mother drives her absolutely crazy with her constant meddling. Hell, as a matter of fact, so does my own mother.

"I also thought that we all could have lunch together Saturday or Sunday."

"First, Mary Ann, you really have to talk to Kristen about it. If you want to learn all about insurance policies, I could help; otherwise, wedding stuff is Kristen's expertise, not mine. Second, I'm not going to the coast this weekend. Kristen is going Thursday, so I won't see her until Monday morning when she gets home."

"Are you telling me that my daughter is going out of town without her husband? Hmm, what's that all about? It doesn't look good for a married woman to travel to another state unaccompanied, James. What will people think? Besides, it seems like a great time for the two of you to work on giving me some grandchildren. I know your mother feels the same way, James. We are long overdue to become grandparents."

"Mary Ann, I appreciate your concern, but *another state* is only an hour and a half away. I don't think the *people* will be concerned with Kristen's travel arrangements or chaperone situation. This is an event for her business, and Misty will be joining her Saturday."

Mary Ann pushes on. "Well, dear, it's your decision to make. It just doesn't seem right that your wife will be gone for several days before her business partner joins her when she has a perfectly capable husband to fill the companionship role. Oh well, I guess you're both adults, but this sort of thing would never happen between John and me. We always put our marriage first. Also don't wait too long to start having babies. Kristen isn't getting any younger, you know."

Kristen would be so pissed if she knew her mother just said this to me and is pushing the baby issue again. Now is definitely NOT the time to start talking babies.

"Once again, thanks for calling, but you really need to talk to Kristen about admission. I've got to run. Take care, Mary Ann." *Damn, I've got to give Kristen a heads-up about why her mother is trying to get in touch with her.* I dial her phone number, but the call goes straight to voicemail. It's getting harder and harder to get in touch with my own wife. I shoot off a quick text, instead.

James: Hey, your mother called my office because you're not answering the phone. She wants to know how she can get admission to the bridal show for herself and a few ladies. Rose told her it's not open to the public, but you know how she is…determined to get what she wants.

I decide to leave out the whole *It's time to have babies* comments for both of our sakes.

James: By the way, why is your phone going straight to voicemail?

One hour later…

James: Are you really that busy you can't send a quick response?

Another hour later…

James: I'm starting to think your mother is not the only person you are trying to avoid.

What's up with her? Maybe this is payback. Ah, that's it. She's showing me what it feels like to not have your calls answered. Two can play that game. I'm not trying again. We'll talk this evening.

***

Apparently he's not going to let up. I'll give a quick reply.
Kristen: OK. Got your message. Super busy. Working late. Don't wait up.

Why doesn't he leave me the hell alone? *Go play with your new girlfriend, James.* I need to clear my head. If I can just avoid him until I have the time, privacy, and silence to process this mess, I can come back with a game plan. Until then I don't owe him a damn thing. He has no right to demand immediate responses from me. He can just wait until it fits into *my* time line.

***

Her behavior is weird, not like her at all. She's not the standoffish type. *Is Mary Ann putting doubt in my mind about Kristen's reasons for leaving early? Is my own guilty conscience playing a part?* Insecurity has never been a trait I entertained because I know that worthless shit will just eat you alive if you let it. I'll just have to keep an eye on that.

Busy or not, we stopped making each other a priority. It all seems so nonchalant—one day you're each other's world, and the next you can't even respond to a fucking text! Indifference settles in somewhere along the way. Call me a hopeless romantic, but I want to see the light in my wife's eyes when she looks at me filled with devotion and hot desire, the way she used to.

I can usually find solace in music, like confiding in a best friend. Music has always played an important part in my and Kristen's relationship because of its relatability to our life experiences. No genre was preferred; we loved it all. I hit the play button to initiate my playlist entitled "Kristen," a catalog of all the songs that remind me of her and our journey together, and the lyrics to "Said I Loved You…but I Lied" flow smoothly from the speaker. It immediately transports me back to five years ago to the Beau Rivage. I vividly recall one of my favorite memories, one that I've replayed often about my wife, as the song plays on and resonates with how I feel about her.

We had just enjoyed the love songs belted out by Michael Bolton at the Casino, both feeling horny after hours of taking in his seductive sound. Concerts were one of our favorite things to do, and this one found us professing and reaffirming our commitment and deep love for each other. We were on top of the world, the "It" couple, finding success in all realms of life. We sipped whiskey and danced all night in that hotel room, strengthening our unbreakable connection. It was an emotional night combined with some of the best sex we've ever had. I remember it like it was yesterday.

***

"Hey, baby, hurry back, the concert's about to start."

"I'll be quick, James, this drink is running right through me. I'll get us each another round after I visit the ladies' room."

I watched Kristen walk toward the exit sign and thought, I mean really thought, about how deeply I loved her. She was my world…my everything. I couldn't help but notice the heads turning from male concertgoers as she passed them by with the innocent, natural sway of her hips. No doubt she was a beauty and a great catch! Kristen's mother, Mary Ann, might have been the beauty queen in her day, but Kristen was simply gorgeous and *my* beauty queen. As far back as high school, I was always mesmerized by her big brown eyes that held so much expression, and I recalled having to look away at times so she wouldn't notice what those eyes did to me. It was apparent in my crotch too. She could have easily won pageant titles if that was her thing, but unlike Mary Ann, Kristen never sought out constant attention. Still, to me, she was the most beautiful woman in the world, and I intended to always show her how much she meant to me—physically *and* emotionally.

Ten minutes later, just as the lights begin to dim, Kristen returned with fresh drinks and a welcome-back kiss for me. *What a lucky man I am!* One song after another, we held hands, sang along to each other, and at times she rested her head on my shoulder as I ran my fingers through her dark hair, an intimate act and personal favorite of hers.

Nothing can compare to a live performance. You can just feel the music deep in your bones, internalizing it.

Listening to passionate love songs flawlessly delivered and cozying up to my wife started the evening off right. When the concert concluded, and we were sure Michael Bolton wasn't returning for another encore, we headed out of the arena and into the casino toward a bar where more live music was playing. Rather than taking a seat, we approached the bar, and each ordered two more drinks to go.

I believe we would have had sex right then and there in the elevator riding up to our hotel room, but our hands were occupied with the whiskey glasses. There she was, giving me those seductive "fuck me" eyes, and I didn't need convincing. I knew this woman was all mine—heart, body, and soul—and I could never get enough of her.

The hotel room located on the ninth floor was mildly dark upon entry, except for outdoor lights from nightlife activity below softly peering into the full-length windows.

I quickly found a playlist to fit the mood, "Sexy Soul," hoping to hear the velvety sounds and lyrics of Barry White and Luther Vandross. Sips taken, glasses placed on the dresser, and hands freed, the exploration began. I took Kristen's face in my hands, and she looked directly into my eyes, melting me with her soft, trusting expression. "I love you with everything I have, Kristen."

"I love you, too, James, so much. Now quit yapping and fuck me already!"

Now that's my girl. My mouth crashed into hers while my hands moved over her shoulders and breasts with the eager intensity of a desperate man. I hungered for her feel and her touch. We had all night, but I needed to explore and make love to my wife right then. Reaching to pull off my shirt, she followed suit and removed hers. We kissed and fondled each other, removing our jeans in the process and sliding toward the massive window. We didn't care who could see as Kristen stood before the glass nine stories up and planted her hands against the glass as I stood behind her. She was so beautiful in the soft-colored light shining from down below. I reached around and gently ran my hand between her legs over her panties, seeing her arousal reflected in the glass, before positioning my fingers beneath the elastic. Shock waves ran through me with the first feel of her bare, satin-smooth mound. With one hand in her panties, and the other cupping her breast, I toyed with her attentive nipple, keeping steady eye contact. My gliding fingers dove into the deep folds, steadily skimming her exposed clit; I was so turned on, randomly dipping into the "honey pot," and she rocked, then bucked her hips in response.

My happy, rock-solid dick with a mind of its own stood proudly at attention as Kristen reached behind to grab and stroke it rhythmically, perfectly squeezing from tip to shaft. "Baby, you need to slow down, or I won't be able to last much longer," I pleaded.

In an instant, she whipped around and dropped to her knees, saying, "This is just the beginning of a long night; we're just getting started." Taking me into her mouth's full capacity, she licked and sucked, and damn, I loved fucking her mouth. The best part of it all was the view—my wife's reflection, her bobbing head and sexy, glistening backside as she openly displayed her love and desire for me. I savored and banked that incredible mental image. The urgent need to reciprocate consuming me, I flipped her onto her back and began alternating between lips and tongue to tease and pleasure because I knew that oral sex was another personal favorite of hers. Seeing my face between her legs, gently working her little jewel was enough to drive her crazy, which in turn drove me crazy. She pumped my face. I ground the carpet in response. We climaxed together—hers on my tongue, mine emptied onto her bare thigh. It

JEANNE MCCURLEY

WAS just that—the beginning of a long night of ecstasy routinely replicated every time we stayed at the Beau Rivage, always requesting a room on the ninth floor because we "preferred the view."

***

I make myself stop reminiscing right there. Why torture myself with glimpses of the past that exist no more? Snapping out of the memory, I come to my senses, back to the current moment where I'm losing grip on something I held so dear. Here she is, going without me to the exact location that meant so much to us as a couple and having no trouble doing so. She didn't even let me know she was going early, much less invite me to come with her. She's not giving a second thought to the significance of the location while I sit here struggling to suppress the loss of intimacy we created there in the not-so-distant past. How can she disregard the symbolism of the hotel where our connection deepened, elevating our marriage from good to great? The place where we let music enhance every bit of the experience uninhibited?

Or maybe that interpretation is one-sided. Apparently she is no longer interested in recreating our ninth-floor scene. Unable to solve the mystery for today, I simply settle for acceptance of that which I cannot control. That's what creating memories is for, I guess. Just to have a fond memory to recall someday, right? Besides, I shouldn't feel shunned by her secrecy when I'm keeping secrets of my own.

Maybe I'm a man who's worried about the hazards of a midlife crisis. I hear that's a real thing. Apparently the fire that once occupied her eyes is extinguished, put out, darkened, and I find it difficult to fight for its reignition. I just don't know where we went wrong. I need to feel alive again. Reaching into my jacket, I pull out the piece of paper handed to me today by Cassidy Laine. Now that's a special gal—bright, assertive, and beautiful to boot. She's knowledgeable and obviously skilled at navigating in a man's world. I was captivated by every word expertly delivered. With just this one meeting, I have more than enough confidence in her *abilities*. She wrote her name, address, and cell phone number and seemed pretty excited about getting together again.

This is one piece of paper that must be kept hidden. Keeping secrets has never been my thing, but I know if it gets discovered, everything will be ruined for sure. Now more than ever, I'm feeling the pressure of making a move into another phase of my life that I'm hoping will bring fulfillment. Cassidy may just be the person to help me out of this rut.

Chapter 5

I was the first to arrive at Formal Affairs Thursday morning, sneaking out of the house while James remained asleep. I've avoided interactions for the most part, and when unavoidable, I deliver an Oscar-worthy performance. But hell, I'm no actress, no marriage counselor, no psychologist, and obviously no happily married woman. At this moment, I'm just a gal whose heart is being ripped apart, seeking a little solitude to determine my next moves.

Damn, whose keys are jingling at the door already? Can't a girl get some meditation time? We're not due to open for another two hours! I plaster on my "I've got my shit together" face but breathe a sigh of relief and dismiss the phony spectacle when Misty enters the etched-glass doors.

"What are you doing here so early?" I demand of Misty.

"What in the hell do you *think* I'm doing here so early? I'm supporting my best friend. I didn't dare call or send you a text last night. I don't know what control James has over your phone, or if he'd pick it up and scroll through it when you weren't looking. So here I am, needing an update. Spill. Here," she says, handing me a piping-hot skinny mocha latte, "I brought you a little pick-me-up."

"Well, my friend, you can join me for the great reveal. I was able to install the spyware on James's phone after he fell asleep last night. I obviously can't trust him, so this will tell me everything I need to know."

"How does it work? What's the chance he finds out about it?" Misty asks, puzzled.

"The program runs in the background, recording every conversation on his phone. Each day I get an email of the conversations perfectly transcribed right before midnight. Since I just installed it last night after the dinner, I should have received an email with every verbal conversation and text message sent and received to his phone number. Let's see.

"What time did you install it?"

"It was about ten p.m., right before I jumped in the shower. It took less than five minutes to install. I know he was sleeping because he was snoring. Logging into my email account, I retrieved an email sent at 11:55 last night from the spyware. Looks like texts were sent—*What the hell!*—at 10:27 p.m.!"

"Kristen, he must not have been sleeping! He knows you did something to his phone!"

Reading through the messages, my worst fears are becoming my new reality. "No, Misty, he doesn't suspect a thing." Heart sinking once again to the pit of my stomach, a sea of warm tears is unleashed. I toss my phone as I walk toward the bathroom to retrieve a tissue.

James: Hey, I only have a minute. Kristen's blow-drying her hair. She's going out of town tomorrow and won't be back until Monday morning. Do you want to meet Friday or Saturday? I don't want to wait until Sunday in case she decides to return early.

Laine: That would be perfect. Where and when? I'll be back in town this weekend. I already have a reservation at the Hilton. Why don't we just meet there?

James: OK. Let's do Friday night at 7:00. Don't text anymore tonight; she'll be out of the bathroom soon. I'm looking forward to meeting up Friday.

"Who in the hell is Laine?" Misty is mad as she addresses me. "Is that some sort of code name? You must have woken him up with the blow-dryer. That's the only thing that makes sense. And you're right; he has no idea you put that on his phone."

Taking a deep breath and dabbing the tears at my eyes, I feel defeated. "I guess I was hoping that the spyware would prove me wrong. Instead it just confirmed what I already felt inside. My husband is planning to meet a woman at her hotel. What am I supposed to do with that, confront him? Show him the recording of his conversation? Go out of town and make it convenient for him to fuck another woman? Damn, Misty, I can't believe this is happening to me, and I have proof of it in black and white."

"I'm an awful friend. I know you're devastated, and I don't know how to guide you right now. I want you to shove it in his face, but we need to think this through. Think about the repercussions either way. By the way Mike told me that they are catching a football game on Saturday and grabbing a few drinks, so I know he won't be with her on Saturday.

"Yeah, I'm sure that's why he confirmed for Friday night. Gee, that's supposed to make me feel better? 'Great, my husband won't be sleeping with another woman Saturday night because he already took care of that on Friday night!' I've never heard him mention a Laine before. It's got to be a fake male name that wouldn't cause me to be suspicious." Another heated wave of emotional hurt intensifies, making my face flush and my hands shake. I physically struggle to manage my emotions.

"Do you want me to spy on him Friday? I can go by the hotel in disguise and maybe even snap some pictures."

Emotions overcoming me, I feel like I'm suffocating and can barely form the response, which sounds like I'm stuttering. "That won't help M-Misty; we both know they won't be out in public. He's going to have s-sex with that woman in her h-hotel room. Why am I not enough? Why is our life together n-not enough?"

"I can't bear to hear this. Snap out of it, Kristen, you've done nothing wrong. You've been the perfect wife to him. I have been there with you from the very beginning, and I won't let you question your devotion or blame yourself for his deceptions. I asked Mike if he thought James had been acting weird lately, but he said no. I told him I thought the two of you might be going through something. Mike said guys don't talk about that kind of stuff, but he thought James was being his usual self. No red flags. I asked him not to mention anything, that it was just a hunch. Don't worry; he won't bring it up. He literally told me to mind my business."

There's a knock on the glass doors that startles us, or should I say scares the crap out of us! Misty says, "Hurry, fix your face, and I'll see who's at the door." Pulling myself together, I spot Dreamy Chad coming in with a package.

"Chad, what are you doing here so early? I ask.

"I could ask you both the same question, ladies. We're pretty backed up with deliveries, so the drivers were offered overtime to come in early and stay late to catch up. I jumped on it because the pay is really good. By the looks of things here, it seems like I just missed the showing of a sad movie or something. Kristen, are you OK? It looks like you were crying."

I open my mouth to speak but am instantly interrupted by Misty's protective nature. "No, Chad, we were just having girl talk. It's no big deal. I'm sure you've heard that when girls talk, things can get emotional. Sometimes we get drunk, sometimes we curse like sailors, and sometimes we just cry it out."

Turning to face me, Dreamy Chad comments, "Well, Kristen, if any mean girls come here to pick a wedding dress and try to bully you for a discount, I'm just a call away. I feel like a big brother to y'all, being how I delivered Formal Affairs's very first package before the doors even opened on day one. I have a stake in this company's success, too, you know. It's job security for me. No other business in town receives more daily packages."

I'd never considered that Dreamy Chad had been with us from the beginning. Actually he's been much more than our package delivery guy, and I hope we have treated him as such. Now I question that and search his expression for confirmation. Chad had been friends with James and

Mike, annually participating in their football league draft event. When he learned that their wives were opening a bridal boutique that would entice commerce to the area and, of course, more ladies, Chad had selflessly volunteered to help with the renovations. I guess he's so comfortable here because he manually built part of this place. Dreamy Chad, such a fitting name for a total hottie, never divulged much about his personal relationships, just that he wasn't interested in a long-term relationship. Perhaps he suffered a broken heart along the way, or maybe he thinks maintaining a relationship would require too much time and energy. Who knows? He seems to have mastered the art of secrecy regarding his personal life, always deflecting questions and inserting a joke.

Chad was always the proper gentleman, even when Sunny swooned over him and told him dirty jokes. He would simply laugh, or say, "That's a good one," before saying, "I'll see you ladies tomorrow." Sunny would retreat with disappointment on her face. If Dreamy Chad would simply give her the tiniest indication of interest, she would ride him wildly for hours and share every detail, like a teenage boy with his locker-room buddies. It would be a perfect match because, like Chad, Sunny never wants to settle down with one man. She's even said, "With all the hunky men with chunky dicks, why would I pick just one when I can feast on them all!" Jesus, she's such a funny little whore. That's our Sunny.

"OK, ladies, I'll leave you to your gossip, or conversation, or storytelling…whatever it is." Shaking his head, he adds, "I'll never figure out why women need to confide everything in each other and then cry over it, but then again I'm not a chick. I'm just the good ole delivery guy who'll return tomorrow with a truck full of packages for you lovely ladies."

I speak sincerely to Dreamy Chad. "You're so much more than that to us. You're like family, Chad. We really care about you."

He grins and starts laughing. "If you really want to treat me like family, keep Sunny away from me. That girl has got to have some type of STD that she would love to share with me!" We all laugh. "Seriously, though, Sunny's a great gal, but she's not my type. If you could drop that hint without hurting her feelings, I'd appreciate it."

"Sure thing," Misty responds. "Maybe I'll warn her that you're such a player that it's *you* who probably has an STD!" Again the laughter lightens the mood.

As Dreamy Chad heads toward the doors, he turns back and looks directly at me with a serious glare. "For real, Kristen, if you ever want to talk or hang out, I'm a phone call away." With that, he winks and exits the doors, leaving Misty and me speechless with dropped jaws.

"What the hell was that?" Misty exclaims. "Dreamy Chad totally checked you out! He looked you up and down and winked at you. Why would he extend an open invite like that when he knows you're married? He's even friends with James!"

"Oh no, Misty, do you think Chad knows that James is cheating on me? They *are* friends, and James *was* out in public, not hiding his affection for another woman—*Laine* to be exact. This is so embarrassing. I wonder how many other people saw them together. Tuesday was the first time *we* saw them, but how many times has he been out in public with her? Ugh! I could crawl under a rock and die right now!" OK, I must admit that the way Dreamy Chad just looked at me and winked made me feel a certain way—not sure what way—but I definitely have goose bumps on my arms. Maybe he sees a marriage heading toward its demise, and he wants in on its ruins? Good Lord, I can't think about this right now.

Misty is looking at me with raised eyebrows and a dirty little grin. "Girl, if James is cheating on you, why not explore that sexy specimen of a man who just pictured you undressed? We all know Dreamy Chad doesn't kiss and tell. He's like a vault."

I scold her, "You're absolutely right; you are NOT being a good friend to me! How can you suggest I cheat on James just because he is cheating on me? I already told you I need to figure out what to do from here. I can't complicate matters for revenge sex. If James and I go our separate ways, there will be plenty of time for that!"

"I'm sorry," she says. "I should have never said that. It was insensitive of me to make light of your situation. I'm on Team Kristen all the way. Just let me know how I can help and I'll be there."

"It's just that I never imagined being in this position at this point in my life. I feel like the world is spinning around me while I stand here frozen. I'm still in shock, I'm extremely hurt, I'm so sad that James doesn't respect our marriage, and I feel that I have no control over the situation. I'm losing my grasp on the man I've always loved. All I know is that I have a lot of thinking to do. I still haven't processed the magnitude of the betrayal or evidence and how it's going to impact my security moving forward. Look, Misty, I'm going to be in the office for a little while. I can't be out here when Sunny and the others arrive. My despair is written all over my face. I see it in the mirror, and I really don't want to answer any questions, so cover for me, OK?"

"You got it, girl. I'll tell everyone you came in early to take care of paperwork and payroll items and that you're not to be disturbed."

I whisper the words *thank you* and walk to my office. Taking a seat behind my cherrywood desk, I take in my surroundings. Every object represents a symbol of my life with James, whether it's the floral painting we picked up on a special vacation to Venice, the engraved teakwood box holding my desk key and love notes that he had specially ordered with my new monogram when we got married, or the Persian rug he bought me to fancy up the space. I clearly see James's gorgeous green eyes peering directly into mine from the picture frame. I turn it over, facedown, and let the waterworks fall again. *Why is he doing this to me? To us?*

I cry freely for about fifteen minutes before reaching to turn on my computer screen. It's then that a message catches my attention. It says to please call Drew, and a phone number is listed. *Who is this Drew guy, and why is he trying to get in touch with me?* The message was taken again by Sunny, who wrote at the bottom, "This guy called again and only wants to talk to you. I was lucky to get his number." Deciding that sitting in this office is mental torture, I type a text to Misty.

Kristen: I cannot sit in this office anymore. Everything reminds me of James. It's like I'm struggling to breathe. Please take care of the payroll for me.

Misty: No problem. I've got it covered.

I grab my purse, along with the message and the remainder of my pride, and exit out the back door.

FORMAL AFFAIRS

At least I am now safe in my own car, free from spectators who will express concern. These are my friends. Friends who will see sorrow seeping from my skin or hear anguish in my words and want to help, except they can't. I have about an hour and a half to get lost in my thoughts without peering eyes, and I take full advantage of the whooshing highway sounds and random bumps in the road to provide a calming distraction. This doesn't last long. The emotional roller coaster is back, and I begin contemplating all sides of my situation.

We made a commitment; we took vows. Apparently only one of us remembers that. Images of divorce court, property ownership battles, financial woes, and utter embarrassment and betrayal instantly flood my thoughts. I need to thoughtfully weigh my options, plan for my next steps, and control this situation myself. I refuse to be infidelity's pitiful victim.

Will we end up divorced? Of course this is one real possibility. Divorce is a dirty word in my family. To even consider the word, much less mention it out loud, deems me a common gutter rat in terms of my position on the family tree. I don't want to leave him just to spite my bitchy mother, but her resulting disapproval makes it just a little sweeter. Maybe she would finally recognize that I am my own woman. Yeah, that's right, I said *woman*. I'm not the little girl seeking her approval anymore, fearful of disappointing her. Maybe I need to be more unbiased about our mother-daughter relationship. Should I try to talk to my mother about this? Maybe she would be open-minded and offer impartial guidance. Maybe she would empathize with her only child, her daughter, who has demonstrated complete loyalty to her views for a lifetime. After all, she *is* my mother.

Ha! Not in this fucking lifetime!

Could I ever imagine forgiveness as a possibility? I'm not sure I have the strength to do it. That is if he even wanted to work on it. But wait, why should it be his decision anyway? *I'm* the victim here. Shit, I can see myself headed straight to therapy. That thought is interrupted by the ding of an incoming text on my cell phone.

James: Hey, baby, I haven't heard from you today. When are you getting on the road?

This motherfucker is relentless! I know he's just texting to confirm my whereabouts. He's being a sneaky rat. I choose not to respond. Within ten minutes, the phone starts ringing. I choose not to answer. I get another text.

James: Kristen, what's going on? Why won't you answer me? I called the shop, and Sunny said you left a little while ago. Is everything OK?

Ding. Another text is coming in.

Misty: You better answer James. He already called the shop and then my cell phone. I had to tell him you

already left. He said if he doesn't hear from you, he's driving to the Coast to come find you.

Kristen: Got it. I'll respond to him.

I dial his number. He answers right away.

James answers angrily, "Where the hell are you, Kristen?"

I respond coolly, "You don't have to track me down as if I'm a child. I told you exactly where I was going today."

Still angry, James asks, "What's going on with you? Why didn't you tell me you were leaving? We don't go out of town without telling the other goodbye."

"Well, James, it appears there're several things we don't do anymore, but you don't see me calling all over town about it. Look, I'm going to this bead store appointment and attending the show this weekend. And truthfully I'm just looking forward to a little me time. Can't you understand that?"

"Why? Why do you need to be alone? Since when do we do 'me' time, Kristen?"

Sarcastically but still in a cool tone, I retort, "Don't worry, I won't expectantly return home and mess up any weekend plans you have."

"What are you talking about? I'm just having a few beers with Mike for the LSU game Saturday. I don't have any other plans."

Liar, liar, oh motherfucking liar! I strum up the biggest bit of courage to sound normal and get the hell off the phone.

"OK. Look, I'm pulling up at the gas station to fill up. We'll talk later. Enjoy the game."

"Wait! Wait just a goddamn minute. It's only Thursday. The game isn't until Saturday. Are you planning on not talking to me for the next few *days*? Come on, Kristen. There's more going on than you needing 'me' time."

"Can you just please give me some space? That's all I'm asking for. I need some damn space, James!"

"To be clear, I'll give you some damn space if that's what you *really* need, but I'll be waiting to hear from you."

"I'm sure you'll find something to occupy your time." I end the call and pull off the highway to compose myself.

Chapter 6

I was a fool to think I could actually get any work done today with this massive headache and knot in my stomach. My appetite hasn't been the same either since I met Cassidy Laine. I'm trying to play this as cool as I can, but it feels like I'm losing this balancing act. I don't know if I'm fooling anyone with my attempt at a poker face or not. I'm just not the best at keeping secrets, especially from Kristen. I'm constantly walking on eggshells, trying to get a read on her, and her new dismissive attitude leaves me unsure whether or not suspicions exist. Glancing at my calendar, oddly enough I have no appointments scheduled that could divert my mind from wondering about the what-ifs. I'm consumed in thought when Rose appears in the doorway, startling me back to reality.

"Good morning, James!" she exclaims in a much happier tone than I feel like dealing with at the moment. She crosses into my office, uninvited of course, with a coffee mug and places it on my desk. Whenever Rose brings me coffee, or a muffin, or anything for fuck's sake, she's usually on a fact-finding expedition. I sit up straight in my chair and prepare for what's coming.

"I didn't see you walk to the coffeepot yet, so I thought I'd save you a trip and bring some to you."

"Thanks, Rose, but that's really not necessary. I already had a cup at home this morning, but I'll take this one since you went through the trouble of making it. I don't want you to wait on me, Rose." The look on her face reads as if I had just told her that her puppy had died. The strong stench of granny perfume wafts toward me, suddenly making the fresh scent of coffee nauseating as they mix. She lifts her drawn-on eyebrows and purses her orange-lined glossy lips before reading me the riot act.

And she begins, "James, you know you're like a son to me and Henry, and your parents are our dearest friends. I don't mind serving you, sweetie; we're all *family* after all. You know I look after you as if you are my own child, and if you don't mind me saying, I've noticed you've been bothered by something lately. A little, um, preoccupied if you will."

Great. This is just what I need, another mother figure meddling in my business. Instead of telling her where to keep her nose—and for the record, that would be out of my business—I mind my manners. "I'm just a busy man who's trying to run a business, Rose. Thanks for the concern, but it's truly not warranted. And"—taking a sip of the piping hot java—"this coffee is especially tasty this morning. You must have the magic touch!"

"Well, dear, I'm not one to pry, but I couldn't help noticing a little tension between you and Kristen at dinner a few nights ago. I'm hoping everything is OK between the two of you?"

Damn, these southern women are relentless with their intrusiveness. They come at you as if you're an idiot and can't see through their dialect and nosy line of questioning. They use their caring nature and phony "concerned for you" comments to their advantage. They weaken your exterior barriers and go straight for the jugular. Stab, stab, stab until they wrench the information out of you, leaving you to completely bleed out and unaware of what just hit you.

"I assure you that everything is fine. Again, thanks for the concern," I tell her as I rise and grab my keys. "I'll be out for a couple of hours. I don't have anything pressing on my agenda for today, so I'll see you later."

"But where are you going? There's nothing on your calendar."

This woman will not stop with the damn questioning. "I have a personal errand to run," I say as I slide past Rose and direct my attention to the elevator. Feeling her eyes still on me, I opt for the stairs while turning my head back to say, "Thanks again for the coffee."

What in the world is going on with Kristen? Is she already checking out? If so, is it because she's over *us*? Or does she suspect what I'm up to? She has been making snarky remarks lately, implying that I'm preoccupied or disinterested. Either way, I need an accurate account of where her mind is, and I know just how to find out…Misty.

Driving over to Formal Affairs, unexpected rain starts pouring, beating angrily on my car's hood. Thunder erupts in loud crashes nearby, and lightning strikes encompass the sky. This is what my life feels like currently, a giant mess of a despicable thunderstorm. And no end in sight. I turn up the radio's volume because I can hardly hear it over the pelting raindrops and decide that was a mistake. Kristen's favorite wedding song of all time, our first dance ballad, "We've Only Just Begun" by the Carpenters, is playing, and it takes me back to that special day.

Tiny details fade with time, but I clearly remember watching Kristen slowly walk down the aisle toward me, ready to become my wife. I memorized every move, every expression. She was absolutely stunning and had the happiest, most content look on her face. It was the look I'll never forget. Everything I could have ever hoped for was revealed in her expressive eyes; they held so much. With every step taken, she was seconds closer to becoming my wife. She was my future, my world.

The lyrics play on about a couple just starting life's journey together, so full of promise and commitment. Hard *Click*. I can't listen to this anymore. We are so far removed from that time. We've slowly evolved into mere coexistence, and my focus must change.

I think about sending Misty a text to let her know I'm coming but reconsider doing that. She needs to be caught off guard. I don't want to give her time to concoct some story or even let Kristen know that I'm on my way. If there's anything I'm sure of, it's that if Kristen is up to something, then Misty knows about it. True partners in crime, those two.

Due to the bad weather, it takes me a little longer to arrive, but I see Misty's SUV in the parking lot of Formal Affairs, so I'm sure she's there. The parking lot is mostly full, even for a rainy day, so I'm prepared for her to tell me she's too busy to talk with me. I won't accept that. Damn, it's really pouring out here, but there's no time like the present to put Misty on the spot. I make a mad dash to the shop, and as I ascend the porch steps and reach for the glass door, a young man comes out, and says, "Excuse me, James," as he climbs down the steps. It hits me as I hurry out of the rain and enter the building that I don't recognize him. *How does he know my name?*

Misty is assisting a customer but immediately spots me. She excuses herself, approaches me, and asks, "What are you doing here? I told you earlier that Kristen has already left." She seems very cautious about my presence there.

"I know it's the workday, and you've got customers to tend to, but I really need to talk to you."

"You've got that right," she says. "I'm pretty busy right now. I can call you later."

"Misty, this will only take a few minutes," I reply as I lightly grab her arm and lead her down the hall toward the offices. "By the way, who was that guy that just left? He addressed me by name, but I don't recognize him."

"I don't know him either. His name is Drew, and he left a couple of messages for Kristen over the last week, but I don't think she knows him either. He won't talk to anyone else. She thinks he's probably a vendor or someone seeking a donation or an interview. She grabbed the last message he left when she took off a little while ago. My guess is she'll call him back from the road."

My mind starts spinning with ideas I don't want to entertain at this moment. *Who is this Drew guy? Could Kristen be seeing him, and that's why she's been so distant? It would certainly be convenient for them to communicate through the boutique. Untraceable, easy to cover your tracks.*

We enter Kristen's empty office, and I immediately begin. "Look, I know you and Kristen have been best friends since…well, forever, but I consider you *my* friend too. I need help. I know that if something was going on with Kristen, you would know about it. She would confide in *you*. But you've been with us—both you and Mike have been with us through the ups and downs—our very best friends, and I need you to help me reach her."

"James, if you're trying to reach her, call her cell or the hotel room. She'll be checking in soon, I'm sure."

"Not *that* kind of reach, Misty. I need to know and understand whatever she's going through so that I can be there to help."

"Help?" she asks in a sarcastic tone with a hand on her hip. *Can he seriously be standing here expecting me to betray my best friend, the person he is apparently cheating on? Destroy her trust like he's doing? No, he's just fishing to see if I'll let on that Kristen knows all about Laine! I refuse to let him bait me.* "Listen, if there is something going on in your marriage, that's between the two of you, and it's in my best interest not to get in the middle of it."

"Come on, Misty, I know you and Kristen share everything, and I totally respect the 'girls code of honor.' I just don't know what to fix if I don't know what the problem is. I'm not asking you to betray her confidence; I'm just asking for a little direction here…a starting point to possibly fix things before we get to a point of no return."

"Well, all I can suggest is that you really consider what you've been doing and decide for yourself if those actions are in the best interest of your marriage. Other than that I really can't expand on anything," she states as a matter-of-fact, *this conversation is over* tone.

With that, I reach to hug her before I leave, but she pulls back like I have the plague. This is not like her. She's acting like I'm the enemy. So strange. Misty and I have shared many friendly hugs over the years. I just don't understand. "What's wrong, Misty? Did I do or say something to make you uncomfortable?"

"No, no, I just really need to get back to work. You and Mike enjoy the game Saturday." Visibly nervous, she turns, leaving me dumbfounded and alone in the empty office.

Wow, that did not go very well. My suspicions are confirmed—she knows *exactly* what's bothering Kristen, she's not going to open up to me, and I'm *definitely* at fault.

Chapter 7

There's solace in alone time on the open road. There's a quiet peace surrounding me in my car ever since I determined that the radio is not my friend for now. Every song played reminded me of another time in my life when James and I shared everything. I don't need melodic reminders of the past. I fought for this uninterrupted private time, and now that I have it, it's solely mine. I need to consider the fragmented pieces left in the wake of unfaithfulness. *Ding, ding.* Two text messages are coming in. Crap! Did I just say uninterrupted?

Misty: FYI—James just showed up here asking what's wrong with you. I told him nothing. He said he knew that you would confide in me if something was going on, and he wanted to know what it was so he could 'help!' Before cutting the conversation short, I basically

told him that if anything was wrong, he should consider his own actions.

Misty: That guy Drew stopped by. I told him you were out for a few days. He's cute and super polite, whoever he is!

Kristen: Good answer to James. I'll call Drew. Don't let Sunny meet him until we find out who he is! Otherwise he'll be her next conquest, and she could spoil a potential client for us! And if James keeps pissing me off, I may get to know this Drew guy even better. Did he give any other information?

Misty: Not a word. Like I said, he was handsomely attractive and seemed like a nice guy, a gentleman of sorts. You know, clean cut, smelling good, tight and styled hair, very well-manicured and courteous.

Still driving I reach down into my purse to retrieve the message from Drew. I probably shouldn't call from my cell phone in the event this is some creep who will now have my phone number, but I may as well get this call out of the way if I'm ever going to get time to think. The call is answered on the second ring with a manly, "Hello?"

"Hi, may I please speak with Drew? This is Kristen Montgomery returning his call."

"Oh hi, Kristen, this is Drew. Thank you for getting back with me."

Getting right to the point, I say, "Well, Drew, apparently it's more than 'a call.' It's been *several* calls and a few visits to my place of business. How can I help you? Are you a formal apparel vendor?"

"Um, no, Kristen, I'm not. Actually I was hoping we could talk face-to-face."

"Excuse me, do I know you? What is—" I'm cut off midsentence by Drew's intrusion.

"I'm not a vendor, although I do appreciate a nicely tailored tuxedo." He chuckles. "I'm really sorry for trying to contact you so many times, but I have an important personal matter that I believe you can help me with. I know this is an odd request. Would you please agree to meet with me? It can be in a public place around lots of people in complete daylight. I wouldn't expect a female to agree to meet in a private setting."

"Can you tell me what this is in reference to? I'm not in the habit of agreeing to meet strangers just because I'm asked to, *especially* to discuss anything personal." Maybe he's just being a respectful gentleman, but my safety is truly not his concern. Am I giving off a *please protect me, kind sir* vibe? Either way my defenses are on full alert; that is until he recites my name again, and his tone appears to be familiar, rich yet smooth, and I feel like we've met before.

"Kristen, I don't want to get into the details, but it has to do with a possible family connection."

I respond cautiously. "You know, Drew, there is much about my family out there for public viewing on a variety of social media platforms. Have you tried exploring any of those options? Maybe your questions could be answered there?" Let's hope this guy is not just curious about or a stalker of my beauty queen mother and her mild celebrity status or about my father's well-publicized community good deeds and gala events.

"No, it's nothing like that, Kristen. If you'll agree to meet me, I promise to keep it brief and respect your time."

My stranger-danger alert must be malfunctioning today because I'm not automatically saying no. There's something genuine in the sound of his voice, and I don't feel afraid. Against my better judgment, I offer, "Look, Drew, I don't know where you're located, but if Mississippi isn't out of range, I'll be representing my boutique at the bridal bizarre this weekend. The event is being held at the Coliseum on the Coast. That's public enough. I can meet with you before the event starts either tomorrow morning or—" *What's with this guy? He cuts me off again!*

"Tomorrow is perfect! I'll be there!" Drew responds excitedly.

"Well, Drew, where *exactly* is *there*?"

He says, "Wherever you're most comfortable. There are several refreshment centers at the Coliseum. I've been there many times; I'm a local. Actually there's a place with seat-ing close to the main entrance called Dan's Coffee Stand. Does that work for you around ten a.m.?"

"Yes. I'll be there. See you then," I respond, and end the call. What could this guy be referring to by "family connection"? Is he mistaking me for some long-lost cousin? I guess I'll find out tomorrow morning. I'm not wasting any more of my private time thinking about Drew's family when my own is deteriorating by the second.

When did my marriage take a turn toward destruction? I really thought James and I were happy, and for years he never gave me an indication that he was anything but. Would he tell me if that was the case? Or would he simply go through the motions—the mundane routines of daily life—until there was an opportunity for safe escape? A better offer perhaps? Maybe I was blissfully blind or in denial that our marriage could withstand anything. Reality sucks ass, doesn't it? Or does it? Am I seeing what I think I'm seeing from James? His actions have been deceptive. I've caught him in multiple lies over the past few weeks, his staff is covering for him at work while he disappears for intimate lunch dates with Laine, and who knows how many others there are or have been? He's secretly texting while he knows I'm preoccupied with drying my hair or when he thinks I'm asleep, he doesn't answer my calls or texts and then lies about his availability to answer, and he's been so distant. That is except when he wants sex. In those moments he becomes someone else. Someone I hardly know who seems to have to work very hard at convincing himself that he wants me. Will a man's need for physical release mask his disdain for his partner? I suppose I've given him very little encouragement in that area, as it is impossible for me to fake desire for a deceitful husband.

For women—well, at least for *me*—physical desire *never* trumps emotional connection and stability. I have more self-worth than allowing myself to be used for physical gratification by someone who respects me so little. Mother's voice creeps back in, and I hear her distant yet authoritative whispers, "It is a woman's wifely duty to take care of her husband, and if you don't do it, someone else will." He can masturbate day and night for all I care. However, my own eyes have witnessed him flirting with that redhead, so she must be giving him what I can't and won't.

There's still one nagging piece to all of this. With all that I know for sure James has done, I question whether I have enough evidence to take him to the cleaners. I can't stop James from doing what he's doing. What's done is done. I wouldn't want to have to force my husband to stop cheating on me. I can't fit the mold of a submissive, turn-a-blind-eye type of woman; I've crossed over and emerged a strong, decisively proud woman in control of my own destiny. The only way I want loyalty is if it's given selflessly and willingly. He may be stomping all over my dignity, but I must be smart, maneuvering a plan to ensure my financial security. It's not the time to be reactive and let emotions guide my moves. My next steps for the foreseeable future will involve collecting more proof of adultery, and when I am confident that I have a solid case to prove infidelity on James's part, I'll sue him for divorce and collect huge alimony payments for years to come. With that decided, I pull into the parking lot of the Beau Rivage to check into my hotel room, which better be anywhere besides the ninth floor.

My suite and its view are quite lovely as usual. I am happily settling in on the third floor with a plush room overlooking the ocean. The minibar is fully stocked, so I pour myself a full glass of garnet-colored courage, cabernet for starters, and glare from my window into the expansive ocean. Whitecaps from approaching waves crash onto the shore in alternating patterns, leaving the sand to glisten in the golden sunlight. A sense of calm passes over me, sending the slightest tingling sensation down my back. It's a peaceful feeling of inner strength and decisiveness, and I momentarily feel at ease. That is until the mind of this seemingly liberated woman drifts to another time I felt at peace. It was when James and I cruised the Caribbean Islands for our tenth wedding anniversary and fell in love with Jamaica.

Without distraction, we explored the island and each other completely. We made love on the beach inside an enclosed cabana we rented overnight. It was a beautifully magical night, so hot in more ways than one. The repetitive sounds of waves and breeze, combined with live resort music humming in the distance and shimmers of sultry moonlight peeking into the private hut, provided the perfect backdrop for lovers. And that we were, as intimate as two people could be. I vividly remember lying face-to-face as James's strong hands slowly ran along my body, causing goose bumps to appear on my legs. He gently caressed my begging flesh as if he was completely enamored with every part of me, worshiping each individually with lovingly seductive eyes and perfect, tender touch. The way he slowly rolled his tongue over my nipples while fondling the prize between my legs prepared me for entry by his rigid penis. Over and over, he filled me with lust and love, riding out waves of pleasure until we both glistened with sweat and exhaustion.

We were so perfect together. With that stinging memory, a lone tear hits the rim of my wine glass and dilutes my liquid courage.

Chapter 8

The bead store is amazing! There are crystals, pearls, and ornate glass in every size, shape, and color covering garments and valuable collectibles. Upon my entry, I see the sunlight piercing through the display window creating a sparkling prism of lights on every reflective surface. I'm taken aback, as if gazing into a kaleidoscope, entranced by the dancing array of tinted light. Face flushed with wonder, slowly spinning to catch every amazing reflection. The daze is broken by a store clerk offering halfhearted assistance.

"Oh, hi, I have an appointment with Mr. Martin, the shop owner, for five; I'm a few minutes early, so I'll just browse while I wait. But I'm most curious to know how you manage to work here in this fantastic light show? I feel like my senses are on overload; it's quite beautiful!" The apparently annoyed twenty-something rolls her eyes and obnoxiously chomps her visible cotton-candy-pink bubble gum. *She could use a lesson or two in customer service and professionalism, not to mention makeup application,* I think, as I take in that hideous half-inch-thick black eyeliner she must assume enhances her forgettable facial features.

"You get used to it." Her name tag reads "Alexandra," but surely, she is unworthy of such a classy name. "I'll let him know you're here, Miss?"

"Kristen." I clear my throat and adjust my posture, growing an additional inch in height. "Kristen Montgomery. Take your time; I'm in no hurry."

Little Miss Attitude, showing off her cat-itude, scans me up and down, before saying, "Neither is he."

I hear the opening of a door behind Alexandra, and Mr. Martin invites me into the private meeting room. Immediately, and before I focus on the infamous Angelo Rosetti, I'm hit with the glorious scent of expensive Italian cologne. He reeks of masculinity. I lock eyes with the designer, feel the tingle of a thousand goose bumps protruding from my skin, and manage to extend a hand to greet the mysterious stranger with the deep-set dark eyes, slicked-back ebony hair, and a five o'clock shadow that I could lose my identity in. "It's a pleasure to meet you, Mr. Rosetti." Our eyes are permanently locked, never straying as he stands to his feet and lightly brushes his full lips across the top of my hand in one swift but smooth motion. His eyes carefully scale my body, and a sinister little crooked smile sets on those perfect lips, leaving my racing heart audible to anyone within a twenty-foot range. I now fully understand the meaning behind "He undressed me with his eyes!" And I assume the role of willing conquest. *Can a room's temperature be hot and cold at the same time?* My skin is sizzling, but I can't hold back the chill of building pressure and visibly shake under his watchful appraisal of my physical characteristics. Sensing an inappropriate intimacy, Mr. Martin clears his throat and invites me to sit down. The gesture snaps me from the glaring trance, and I'm suddenly able to collect my senses, sitting in the ornate chair that Angelo pulls out for me.

For the next hour, Mr. Martin, Angelo, and I talk about the origins of crystals, the famous celebrities who model Angelo's gowns on the runways of Florence and Polermo, and the demands of his growing fashion empire. It is clearly apparent that Mr. Martin has tired of the detailed stories some time ago and is looking at me as an unwanted intrusion, but my attention never diverts from the lovely sounds of Italian dialect spewing from Angelo's beautiful lips. *Where have those lips been? I'm sure they have graced the anatomy of many young, zesty wardrobe models—too young and inexperienced to appreciate such a cultured lover!*

Mr. Martin looks at his watch, indicating that he is tired of the conversation, and upon cue, Angelo rises and addresses me directly. "Kristen, Mr. Martin has been so kind as to accommodate my company for the last several hours, even before our extended meeting began. While I am most grateful, I feel that I have intruded enough onto his personal time."

"Truly, it has been no trouble. Your business is my business, Angelo," states a somewhat nervous and now fidgety Mr. Martin, fearful of losing the financial prosperity his business can attribute to Angelo's popularity and creativity in the fashion industry.

"Nonsense, we must be going. Kristen, I'd love to learn more about your little boutique. It serves my interest to know more about the buyers who sell my gowns. Mr. Martin is ready to shut down for the evening. May I interest you in a conversation over drinks?" Angelo's invitation is one I immediately accept, although I am struggling not to appear too eager. He tells me he is staying at the Beau Rivage—how coincidental and very convenient—and I confirm I'm staying there as well. We agree to meet in the hotel's bar at 8:00 p.m. Perfect.

This man is a famous designer; I'm sure he's accustomed to fashionably manicured women, and I refuse to disappoint. Back in my hotel, the process begins with a quick shower and the thought, *I'm so glad I brought something great to wear!* I slip into a "fuck me" dress and strappy heels, switch from peach to once again "fuck me" rich red lipstick, fluff and spray my hair, seductively line my eyes, apply an additional coat of mascara, and finally spray my Chanel Mademoiselle perfume in all the right places. Not that I'll be needing it, but it never hurts a girl to be fully prepared. Taking in my mirrored reflection assures me that I am not some weak victim, but rather I'm a woman defined by her own confidence and sexuality. *Sorry, Mom, but I'm tuning out your wretched words of marital advice for the evening!* With that final declaration made, I head to the bar.

Alone in the elevator, James is trying to call me. Oh yeah, for a brief few minutes, I almost forgot that I have a lying, cheating husband. I decide to call him back. Let's get this out of the way so I can enjoy the honest company of an absolutely gorgeous man. "James, I see you just called. Did you need something?"

"Really, Kristen, *did I need something*? How about communication from my damn wife regarding her whereabouts!"

"What in the hell is wrong with you? Again, you know exactly where I am. I told you I had an appointment at the bead store, and I'm back at the hotel. Now I'm meeting a friend for drinks. If you have a problem with that, then it's just too damn bad. I told you I needed some time. Just fucking give it to me! You of all people have a hell of a nerve demanding to know every step I make."

"What is that supposed to mean, 'me of all people'?"

"Just let it go, James. Have yourself a freaking splendid time this weekend. I know you have plans of your own. Don't give me another thought. I'll see you when I see you." Call ended. Cheeks slightly flustered.

Chin up. Shoulders back. Dignity intact. *Tap, tap, tap.* The sharp chanting of my ever-so-sexy stiletto heels on the marble tiles apparently has a personality of its own and is calling attention to my exit from the elevator. Just for fun I toss my hair over one shoulder and add a little extra sway to my hips with each successive stride. "Work it, girl" sounds in my head, and damn if I do feel like a supermodel tonight!

WOW! Come to Mama! Feet crossed at the ankles, expensive suit, white shirt unbuttoned just enough to reveal that masculine chest, Angelo Rosetti leans with one elbow on the bar and apparently a whiskey in his other hand, exuding testosterone from his pores! That is one spicy hunk of man, and that gorgeous male specimen is waiting on little old me, Kristen Montgomery. Sweet revenge is on its way.

Apparently I'm not the only woman eyeing him up. A couple of attractive, barely clothed young girls are trying to engage him in small talk, but he's not biting. This man cannot be tempted with child play. Instead his eyes lock with mine for the second time in mere hours, and I can feel him disrobing me in his mind. What a naughty little smirk crossing his all-too-perfect mouth. He doesn't move to meet me. Instead he takes a long swig of his brown liquor, which I'm confident now is high-end bourbon, and beckons me with his sex appeal. The familiar goose bumps have graced my skin again, and I'm hoping he doesn't notice as I'm now within feet of his personal space. I open my mouth to speak but am interrupted by his strong finger up to my lips.

"Shhhh," he whispers. "Do not spoil this elegant entry with a casual greeting, Kristen. Allow me to take in your beauty without words, for my imagination to entice you to accompany me to the intimate table I have reserved for us." I nod in agreement, speechless, as he grabs my dainty hand in his much stronger, larger one. We walk around the bar, holding hands as if we are more than strangers who met earlier today. "That's a lovely shade of red on your nails. What color is it?" Angelo's curious, suggestive eyes are wandering and inquiring.

Several drops of sweat tingle on the back of my neck, my big doe eyes blinking seductively, as I answer, "I never thought I'd be asked that question. It's a bit embarrassing, but here goes…Slut Red."

"I'm intrigued."

Wow, those are some serious "fuck me" eyes if I've ever seen them.

"Was the color chosen for its name? Are you a naughty girl, Kristen?"

Damn, nothing like being put on the proverbial spot! How do I answer this question? Mr. Rosetti is a certified panty-dropping, seducing, sexual presence, but I'm not exactly a skilled temptress; therefore, I try to calm the beast by steering the conversation away from the raw heat that is quickly building.

"Sir, it may interest you to know that red has always been my favorite color. It's a bold but classy symbol of power. I've always worn it when I needed to make a statement and show that I'm in charge. At my boutique, whenever I have meetings with potential new vendors, I always wear red. It displays my confidence. It also sends the message that I am decisive, and any partnership that I may enter into is just that…a partnership, not a desperate attempt to have a vendor exploit my business. All negotiations will be on MY terms."

"Hmmm…very interesting. This emboldened business owner routine is dependent upon the color red."

Where is he going with this?

"I see red as a symbol, too, a sign of lust and passion. It represents the desires of a sensual woman, a color not to be wasted on anyone who cannot appreciate its fiery, bold intensity."

Now he's fixated on my breasts and not trying to hide it.

"What plans do you have in mind for that red dress tonight? Have you ever imagined experiencing ecstasy in that dress? From a man who knows how to make that happen and wishes to privately enjoy your company? Kristen, I have some sample rainbow crystals in my room if you would like to see them."

His right hand slowly extends into his pocket, assumingly to pay the bar tab, and I catch the outline of an already straining zipper. He slowly turns back to look at me with piercing and sultry bedroom eyes, and says with a daring proposition, "I'm sure you're up for a challenge. No woman would wear a dress like that absent of the power to back it up. Are you ready to deliver that power, Kristen, to freely express your sexuality?" Panicked by what's for sure to happen if I sit there a second longer or make it into the elevator with him, and envisioning Mother's disapproval of my bad-girl misbehaviors, I jump up with all the ferocity of a caged animal and claw for my pretend-vibrating phone. I fake a call and let Angelo know that I have to tend to a family emergency. In way over my head, I hurriedly walk away, pretending to be emotionally immersed in the call as I wave goodbye.

Alone and frustrated in the empty hotel room, a notification alerts me to an incoming email. It's the spyware update from James's phone. Midnight already. He and Cassidy engage in somewhat innocent small talk right up until they confirm their upcoming meeting at Cassidy Laine's hotel room at 7:00 sharp, and he'll bring the bourbon.

Who needs a fucking man? I yell out loud, hating James for everything he's doing to destroy us, angry at Angelo for trying to seduce me so quickly after we met, and now downright pissed off with myself for not taking him up on it. Crying and breathing heavily, I'm emotionally exhausted, flailing and throwing my body onto the bed. If there's such a thing as an adult tantrum, I'm having one. And I deserve to. I spend the next period of time getting myself off, infuriated and unashamed. Satisfied, I look in the mirror at my unrecognizable, almost animalistic features, knotted hair, sweating, and defeatedly whimper, "Fuck you, James."

heading into the shower, I scan the room, and it exposes the remnants of a desperate scene. My partner in crime last night, the sultry red dress that was supposed to bring me luck in the form of hot revenge sex, lies in a wrinkled heap on the floor, having failed in vain.

"You, damn red dress, are not worthy to wash my car!" With a quick scoop, she lands in the little garbage can beside the full-length mirror, from which my ugly reflection glares back at me. As the mirror's endless and unforgiving gaze highlights every one of my faults, I stare it down, scornfully daring it to stop before abandoning the duel, discarding the stained wine glass, tidying up the rest of the room, and hopping into the shower to wash away last night's embarrassing collection of events.

Sporting a black sleeveless sheath finished with a tan blazer and chunky-heeled pumps, I grab my ringing cell phone and am relieved that it's Misty calling.

Misty: Hey, how was your night? Did anything good happen? How was the bead store?

Kristen: I'm on my way to the Coliseum and don't have much time to talk, so here's the short version. The bead store was fabulous; I visited with Angelo Rosetti, who invited me for drinks. We had drinks, and he propositioned me for sex. I almost did, but I didn't. I got drunk in my hotel room by myself, cried myself to sleep, and I'm about to meet Drew. That's the quick and dirty of it all.

Chapter 9

L'Oréal can make all the claims it chooses to about twenty-four-hour long-wearing mascara, but I bear witness to the fact that the shit runs down your face when prompted by angry tears. My morning face tells the story of a cry-all-night heartbreak affair, a misdemeanor of love gone bad. Of course I look like crap. Who wouldn't when the weight of carrying an unbearable heaviness on the brink of combustion, with deception and insecurity leading the way, consumes all thoughts? It's extremely difficult to manage and simultaneously portray yourself as someone you're not, to mold your physical appearance into that of a stage performer, masking and transforming one's true self into a suitable character worthy of delivering what the audience expects. But this is my current mission. Luckily the hotel provides an in-room coffeepot, so I'll start there. Before

Misty: Wait, hold up! What did you just say? You *met* Angelo Rosetti? *The* Angelo Rosetti? Spill the beans, my friend! Damn, I wish I could have found a different sitter for Chloe!

Kristen: He is possibly the sexiest man alive, but I was way out of my league flirting with him. This guy is no amateur. He could literally melt the clothes off you with just one look! We met at the hotel's bar, and he didn't even pretend to be interested in conversation. He started asking questions but turned answers into sexual comments. The way he stared at me—it was like his piercing eyes were burning through my dress, like he already saw what was underneath. It all happened so fast; I was sweating, my head was spinning, and when he invited me to his room to "look at some beads," I panicked and faked an emergency phone call.

Misty: You did *what*? First, I'm shocked that you met him, but the fact that you managed to get an invite for drinks is beyond imagination. And what dress are you talking about, certainly not that little red number I've been dying to borrow?

Kristen: Yep, that would be the one!

Misty: You must have looked like a highly paid escort! Good for you, showcasing all that bravery! I'm jealous. And where does Drew fit into all of this?

Kristen: I called him on the drive over here. Apparently he wants to discuss a possible family connection. So I bet he's going to claim that we share a common Neanderthal ancestor, or maybe our parents may have known each other back in the Great Depression, some crazy story to either get a reference for a job with Dad's latest real estate venture or maybe he's a reporter who wants to do a feature on the history of southern beauty queens and wants me to put him in contact with Mom. Either way he was nice enough on the phone, and I could use a little entertainment this morning, so I'll play along. However, I don't plan to give him more than fifteen minutes. Let's chat later, my friend!

Dan's Coffee Stand is fairly populated, and the bold coffee aroma fills the air as I approach the table of a handsome man who must be Drew based on the fact that he's watching me approach and stands to greet me. *Well, Drew, aren't you a sight for lonely eyes? You're a cutie!*

"Kristen?" the much taller—and, whoa, is he built—hunky man with a million-dollar smile asks.

"Drew, I presume? How did you know who you were looking for? We've never met." Extending his masculine hand for a traditionally formal greeting, I notice that the grip is fittingly firm but gentle. I am also immediately taken aback by the scent of clean cologne that appears to suit this manly man, a strong, broad-shouldered, not-too-flashy guy.

"I recognize you from the magazines. I really appreciate you meeting me today, and as promised on the phone, I don't want to monopolize your day. I realize this was an unconventional request. My name is Drew Hudson. I reside here in Mississippi, and I'm a co-owner of a construction company, much like your own story. My best friend, Luke, and I restore historic homes, so when I saw the before and after pictures of the old home you renovated for your business, I was intrigued and read the article. Please don't be alarmed, I'm not a stalker. However, once I read your story, I had to research more. I felt like fate had led me to that magazine rack on that specific day."

OK, here's where the construction guy prepares to tell me we are kindred spirits so that he can solicit work from Dad. Let the scam begin.

"Look, Drew, I can appreciate a fellow renovator, but what's the point of all this? Are you looking for a job?" I ask, as I am quickly becoming annoyed. He begins to speak but instantly freezes and turns pale as if he's seen a ghost. Standing now and beginning to walk backward, he says, "Excuse me for just a minute; I'll be right back. Please don't leave."

Well, isn't this nice? My day is starting off just as badly as yesterday ended. Last night, I escaped from an Italian horndog, and this morning Mr. Hot Handyman can't get away from me fast enough. I'm guessing he's running to the nearest

109

restroom to either throw up or handle some "tummy issues." I decide to give him ten more minutes, enough time to order and finish a café latte and that amazing cinnamon roll that I spotted in the glass case. Just when I think the day couldn't get any worse, I hear a painfully distinguishable voice calling my name.

"Kristen, oh Kristen dear!" Oh no, I'd recognize that feminine, high-pitched call in any crowd. It's one that I've heard over and over throughout my childhood when I was in trouble and even when I wasn't. It's the "I'm too much of a lady to raise my voice" call. I knew better than to ignore the summons because otherwise it would merely increase in frequency and progressively grow louder. Slowly turning around, I see Mother standing within five feet of me with a scornful expression of disgust. How familiar.

"What are you doing here?" I ask, markedly irritated.

She hurriedly diverts the question, asking, "The more important question is, why are you purchasing that huge piece of sugar? You know what sugar can do to a girl's figure. If you are going to keep James's eye, you had better start eating in a manner more fitting of a trophy wife. And why is he not with you this weekend? I spoke with him recently, and he did not seem too eager to accompany his wife out of town. Is there something going on, and does it have anything to do with the young man I spotted at your table a minute ago? You can never be too careful of possible rumors developing and spreading like a bad case of the flu, Kristen. Of course because you've been ignoring my phone calls, I had to call in a favor to secure tickets to this event. Quite embarrassing, I might add. My friends will begin to think that I have no connections, and—" She does tend to rattle on and on.

I cut her off midsentence as I give a very animated, hardy wave. "Well look over there, the ladies have all gained entry unharmed, and they're looking for you. You should go and meet them; otherwise, they will rush over here and think that YOU are the one buying this evil cinnamon roll!" Now imagine *that* rumor circulating around town! As quickly as she invaded my private moment, she scurries away to reclaim her position as "Queen Bee" among her enamored and loyal followers. Returning to my empty table, I think about the wonderful gooiness of the succulent cinnamon roll that is about to grace my accepting lips and decide that I am going to enjoy it even more just to spite Mary Ann and her "girlish figure" bullshit. Midbite I look up to find Drew returning to the table. He extends an apology and says that he had to make a phone call; I sense this is a lie.

"Look, I only have a few minutes before I have to get signed in at the registration table. Remember I *am* here for business. So what can I—" Again, interrupted.

"As I mentioned, I read your story, and it began to resonate with me. You see while I grew up in Mississippi, I was raised by a loving set of parents, the best anyone could ask for. They are my *adoptive* parents, Audrey and Stanley Hudson, who are now both elderly but still mentally sharp. Growing up, my parents were very forthcoming about the adoption, and they had always told me they would help me find my biological parents if I sought to. It was never my intention, but last Christmas I received a special gift from my parents. It was a genetic testing kit. My mother said that if I was ever curious about my ancestry and possible medical history, this could be a safe option. Well curiosity got the best of me, and I went through the process. It's pretty interesting how they can trace your genetics, build a family tree, and reveal biological relatives, both near and distant, with a small DNA sample."

This Drew still seems to be on the up-and-up.

"I know exactly what you're talking about. I did the same thing about two years ago," I chime in. "The ancestry tests have come a long way in terms of development and accuracy and have grown in popularity too. I found out that my family descends from Eastern Europe, and I've also been able to connect with some relatives I wouldn't have known about without having gone through this process."

"Right, the bad thing about it is that the results are limited, dependent upon the actions of others to take the test and register with the site so that their results can be logged and traced," Drew reports. "Also I'm sure there are cases where people deliberately avoid these types of tracers because they want their information to be kept confidential. You know, in cases of promiscuity that may have resulted in pregnancy. These tests could reveal a whole lot of secret lifestyles and infidelity and could also lead to entrapment, such as bribery, to keep those secrets well hidden."

"True, that's the unfortunate side of this new technology. It's been really nice chatting with a fellow 'tester,' but what does all of this have to do with me, Drew? I feel there is more to this than simple information sharing. Since I'm registered and my genetics are tracked, did my name happen to show up somewhere in your lineage? Did you want to meet to tell me we are fourth or fifth cousins, share a great-great-grandparent, or something like that?" Rolling my eyes and giggling, I say, "Let's get to the point of this meeting. Do you want to exploit a distant 'family connection' to get a job with my father?"

Taken aback and seemingly offended, Drew exclaims, "Seriously, Kristen, is that what you think? That I want to use you to get a job? As I already mentioned, I have a successful and lucrative business of my own. I don't need handouts from anyone, and I do a great job of making my own connections and promoting my own business. In fact, when I initially received my results, I decided to keep them to myself. I had no intention of interfering in anyone else's life, and I held true to that position until I crossed paths with your magazine article. Maybe it was a mistake, but I thought that since you registered and tested, you might be interested in learning about your lineage too. It got me thinking that maybe I should reach out to you. I'm not expecting anything in return for sharing this knowledge with you. The idea of me soliciting a job couldn't be further from the truth, and the only reason I'm not insulted is because you took a chance to meet a perfect stranger. I wanted to tell you—"

Now it's *my* turn to cut *him* off. "What is it, Drew? What has driven you to hunt me down at my place of business, call me repeatedly, and show up at a damn bridal show to get my attention, huh?"

His upright posture slowly deflates, and his head hangs down as if deciding whether or not to deliver a blow to the gut. He pauses for two seconds, raises his head, looks me straight in the eye, and says, "You're my sister."

"You're so full of shit! Why would you seek me out to hand me this load of crap? Am I being videoed for reality television? Or do you make a habit of playing sick jokes on innocent, unsuspecting women? Just because I voluntarily, out of curiosity, took a DNA test doesn't make me a walking target or a naïve victim of shitty stunts for your personal profit!" *Oh no…I haven't logged into the account to check for new relatives in months!* "What is it then, Drew, money? Do you need..."

Drew hurriedly scrolls through his phone, hands it to me, and says, "Here are my results, complete with my family tree."

I snatch it from him, and front and center is my picture, identifying me as a sibling. I quickly scan and see all my familiar relatives. Of course some limbs are missing from my family tree, but those relatives would have had to register to show up. I also scan the page, making sure the website does, in fact, represent the same company I registered with. Suddenly my life flashes before me as a series of lies. "I need a minute," I say, and sit back in the chair. This is a lot to process. I had always wondered if my parents' marriage was as good as Mary Ann portrayed it to be. She always seemed to try extra hard to convince people that she had a marriage worthy of envy. She wants people to admire her, to want everything she has.

I have often seen my father catch other women's eyes. He was, after all, an exceptionally good-looking man, and he knew this to be true. If he hadn't already known this for himself, there was always a line of trifling tramps waiting to profess it to him. Maybe she was dealing with the same type of indiscretions that I'm experiencing now with James but was better at hiding it. She could have been concerned with losing her lifestyle, one that she could not have supported on her own. Avoidance could have been her lifeline. Maybe she was fanatical about her figure and presenting the image of a picture-perfect wife because she felt he could leave her without a moment's notice. Drew, apparently my new brother, allowed me the quiet space to digest what was happening without intrusion, to allow my thoughts to experience a natural progression. We sat in silence for what seemed like an eternity. I saw the cycle of infidelity go round and round in my head and grew empathetic for what Mom had endured with the straying eye of her husband.

Finally I let out a deep breath, and said, "Drew, I had doubts of my own at times about my father having affairs. I guess I can say that I am disappointed but not fully surprised. Of course I'll need time of my own to process what all this means. In the meantime where do we go from here?" I think I'm remaining fairly calm in light of this bombshell he just tossed to me, but he still seems unnerved. *He can't possibly think I'm going to reach over for a hug and say, "Welcome to the family!" What does he expect from me?*

"Kristen, take another look at the results. We do not share a father. Our connection is on the *maternal* side."

Chapter 10

The weatherman reports that it's going to be a beautiful day. I grimace and accept his interpretation with great skepticism as I click the remote control to turn the television off. Having my morning coffee alone is different. It doesn't even taste the same as when I share it with my wife. It's funny how little tidbits of daily life together get taken for granted, and you never realize the meaning and value of special simple gestures, such as pouring freshly brewed coffee into matching mugs, until those opportunities have dissipated. Thinking back, I remember coffee being an important part of the "getting to know you" days, as so much of our time studying and hanging out was at Coffee & Cocktails. I suppose some would disagree with my recent choices, feeling that meeting Cassidy at the very place where my relationship with Kristen grew and deepened was a bit risky; however, the place still holds nostalgic memories for me of better days. I send Kristen a quick text that reads, "Thinking about you." She can interpret that in any way she wants to because, in return, I receive what I expected—a big, fat nothing.

Does she suspect anything? I've been trying not to seem too preoccupied in her presence, but planning and carrying out secret meetings without a spouse's intuition kicking in is a daunting task. It's a game of mental exhaustion and manipulation that leaves me on edge most days. I'm always wondering if I left a clue somewhere or if she can read my mind. Balancing the sport of secrecy is vital to preventing paranoia from easing in. I suppose her being in Mississippi tonight for the bridal show is turning out to be a blessing. She won't search my scheming eyes and won't detect the scent of another woman on my clothing or on my skin. Although to do any of those things, she would have to be present in my near vicinity, and it seems as though the thought is beginning to repulse her. My phone dings in my pocket, indicating an incoming text that I'm positive won't be Kristen. It's from Mike.

Mike: Hey, man, are we still on for the LSU game tomorrow?

James: You bet! They're gonna crush Alabama.

Mike: What do you have going on tonight? If you want to come grab some pizza at my place, let me know.

Misty is going to be busy packing after finishing up payroll, so she'll be late and then occupied. Plus Chloe has been asking about her uncle James.

James: Why is Misty having to do payroll? That's why Kristen went to work early yesterday morning.

Or so I was told. If not payroll, why did she leave so early?

James: Sorry, buddy, I can't make it tonight. I'm having a business meeting with a client that's in town. Give Chloe a big hug and kiss from Uncle James and tell her I will see her really soon. I'll swing by tomorrow morning around 10:00 a.m. Let the tailgating begin! Purple and gold all the way!

Mike: See you then!

Hmmm…what client is flying in for a meeting on a Friday night? I smell bullshit. I'll just take my own advice, the same advice I gave to Misty, and mind my own damn business.

I've even decided to take off work today to avoid the questions from Rose or my dad. Knowing that Kristen is at the show and her mother has called to ask for tickets, she's sure to stick her nose in it. She'll probably invite me over to have dinner with her and Henry but then pout with utter disappointment when I decline the invitation. There's something about the past generation; they take things too personally, almost as an insult if you don't accept their help or share their antiquated opinions. No, rather than have a dull dinner with the friendly old couple, my sights are set on Ms. Cassidy Laine. Until we meet I'll daydream about my expectations for this evening, working out all the specs in my head while I cut the grass and wash my car to pass the time. I'm like a kid awaiting the arrival of Santa Claus.

***

The traffic is extra heavy this evening, driving to Cassidy's hotel. There's a crowd of rowdy twenty-somethings exiting a party bus in the valet parking drop-off area, so I decide to park my car myself. I'd prefer to keep my car keys with me anyway. I stop counting at fifteen young men standing in front of the hotel lobby, apparently part of a festive bachelor party. They're an enthusiastic bunch for sure! Based on the loud laughter and crude comments, the inebriated group is sure to have hefty hangovers in the morning. I chuckle to myself, having experienced that sort of bonding in my younger years as friends got married. In fact, Mike's bachelor party was a blast! A group of us who played baseball in an adult league flew to Las Vegas for the weekend and definitely returned with secrets never to be spoken of again. Ha, the good old days!

I overhear something about strippers, shaking my head knowingly but with approval as I slide past them to the elevator and wait for it to arrive. Those guys are having the time of their lives tonight. *Ding*! With bourbon in hand, the elevator cues that this is the floor where Cassidy and I are scheduled to privately meet for drinks and light food before exploring what she has to offer. My skin tingles with anticipation. There must be more than one bachelor party here tonight because I hear a major celebration coming from the room directly across from Cassidy's. I tap on the door, it opens, and Cassidy appears, immediately embracing me in a hug that catches me off guard. At the same time, the door across the hall opens to let two more guys in, and there stands Sunny in the background, drinking from a bottle of booze while a young man kisses her neck. Her expression appears to be one of wild flirtation, and her eyes are dancing around, not seeming to be focused on any one target. I rush in the door, hoping she didn't get a good look at me, almost pushing Cassidy to the ground. "What's the matter with you?" she yells. "You made me hit the table and spill the drinks I just fixed for us!" she exclaims, irritated.

"I just saw Sunny in the room across the hall. I hope she didn't see me. Her head was partially back, swigging on a bottle. This ain't good; this could be a disaster!"

"And who is Sunny?" she asks. I forgot that Cassidy doesn't know anyone associated with Kristen, so I briefly explain that she works at Formal Affairs. If Sunny recognized me, my cover will be blown. I'm toying with a major catastrophe here. "She's a quirky character but is totally loyal to Kristen for taking a chance on her and fulfilling the role of big sister." None of us know the whole story about Sunny's past—where she's really from, family ties, etc. She's always deflected personal questions and either cracked jokes or changed the subject when anyone exercised curiosity about private matters. We had all just come to respect that she was a crazy character with a wild libido and resolved to accept her as she was. After all, she's never posed a threat to any of us...that is, until now.

Suddenly my excitement for this evening's possibilities is gone, overshadowed by the weight of executing damage control. *What should I do? If I leave now, who knows when the next time will be that I can safely meet up with Cassidy without watchful eyes? Plus if there's a chance that Sunny hadn't seen me, well, I'd be delivering another chance to. On the other hand, if I stay, I need to assume Sunny didn't see either of us, and my secret is guarded. What a dilemma.* Quickly snapping out of my thoughts, I take in the full-length image of the lovely Cassidy, her beaming smile with excitement and the promise of endless possibilities, and my decision is made. Stay I must.

Over the next few hours, Cassidy and I share drinks, stories, and plans for the future. She's so easy to talk to and has limitless ideas in that beautiful head of hers. I'm confident that I chose the right person to "collaborate" with. She's overly attentive and leaves no detail ignored.

Finally on the brink of exhaustion, I'm so pleased. That is until banging, screaming, and the volume of a traveling stampede jolts me back to reality, and I instinctively jump up to open the hotel room door. With Cassidy peering out from behind me, I catch a glimpse of about four guys running down the hall and disappearing into the stairwell for a quick exit. But the scene before me is something I definitely am not prepared for. There lies Sunny, screaming in pain, naked and badly beaten.

Chapter 11

The whining sirens and bright emergency lights zip down the highway. I had covered Sunny with a blanket before the ambulance arrived while Cassidy was interrogated by the hotel staff and tending officers. No matter what events had transpired, Sunny was exploited enough and didn't deserve to be seen unclothed by peering spectators. Instinctively I jumped into the back of the ambulance with Sunny because at this point I am her only friend. I don't even know if she has any family. She can't speak; hell, she can barely moan and has already lost a lot of blood. Her contorted facial features tell the story of massive blows to the jaw, nose, and eyes. I take her hand in mine to assure her she is not alone. I guess this will be the end of my escapades because I will have to account for what I was doing in that hotel room and at the scene of an assault. It may spark the official end of my marriage, but it's still mild compared to what Sunny is going through. Grabbing my cell phone, I try to call Kristen. No answer. I leave a voicemail asking her to call me and saying that it is an emergency. Impulsively, I dial Misty's number, and although it rings seven times before she picks up, she finally does.

"Misty, I know it's late, but it's an emergency. I'm headed to the hospital with Sunny. I don't know all the details yet, but Misty, it looks like she was beaten up pretty badly."

"What? When and where did this happen? How did you find her? Is she OK?" Misty asks.

"Look, I can't get into the details. We're pulling up at Charity Hospital. You might want to get down here," I say. And Misty, would you please call Kristen? She's not answering my calls. This is no time to play games."

The paramedics are met by hospital staff at the emergency room entry as Sunny is wheeled in, covered by the blood-stained blanket. I'm directed to remain in the waiting room to wait for updates. Sitting is not an option. I have too much nervous energy, so pacing back and forth is the immediate way to relieve it. My thoughts are invaded by the series of events that just transpired. *How am I going to explain being at that hotel? Why was Sunny there in the first place in a hotel room with a bunch of drunk guys? I don't recall seeing any other women, but then again I only had a quick glance into the hotel room across from Cassidy's, and*

125

once I saw Sunny, I didn't look any further. I was all about protecting myself. Now I really feel like a creep. Maybe there was something I could have done to protect Sunny instead of worrying so much about my cover being blown. Even if I ever get the chance to explain all of this to Kristen, she will never forgive me for being so selfish and not intervening to save Sunny from this assault.

With no answers to my self-interrogation, I catch sight of my own despicable reflection in the glass and can't bear the sight of the blood-covered, disgusting figure staring back at me. *When had I become such a self-centered asshole?*

Within minutes, a frantic Misty comes running in with a pajama-wearing Chloe thrown over one shoulder. She doesn't notice me at first, but when she does, she darts toward me. By the frantic expression on her face, I'm expecting a screaming reprimand, but I am surprised by her cool tone as she begins speaking.

"Mike's parking the car," she said. "And Kristen's packing up. She's not staying for the bridal bizarre tomorrow. She'll be here in about two hours. James, there's something you should know. A few hours ago, I received a call from Sunny. She had been invited to attend a bachelor party tonight by a guy she was interested in. I didn't get his name, but he was a good friend of the groom-to-be."

A frazzled Mike enters the hospital, and Misty motions for him to sit down and take sleeping Chloe onto his lap.

Misty continues. "She was simply checking in with me because I warned her that it wasn't safe to be the only female at a bachelor party and that nothing good could come of it. Well Sunny being Sunny, she laughed it off but agreed to call me before she drank too much to let me know how things were going and to let me know if she would like me to come and pick her up if the situation became uncomfortable. When she did, she also shared with me that she saw you at the hotel entering a woman's room. I'm not asking for details because, as Mike has told me before, it's none of my business, but Kristen is my best friend and has been for decades, and you've put me in an awkward position. I can't keep this a secret from her. Besides, this wouldn't remain a secret anyway once the official police investigation begins." *At least, that's what I tell him for now. Kristen already knew he was going to that hotel tonight. However, she did not expect this!*

"Let me explain, Misty," I say, ready to come clean to her and Mike. But Mike holds up a hand to cut off my words.

"Look, man," he says, "at this point, considering why we are here, you should probably keep all those details to yourself. Law enforcement is going to want answers, and Misty and I don't want to be involved. We had nothing to do with any of this except to check on a friend having a medical emergency. We don't need to be incriminated, you

127

know how it goes…guilt by association, so it's best if we truly don't know anything or have any details to report. It's probably best for you too. James, we are friends with *both* you and Kristen, and we'd like to keep it that way. Whatever is going on between you two, and it's very obvious that something is, we just want to remain neutral."

"I understand. Kristen and I *have* been going through a rough patch and have a lot to work through. I fully intend to disclose my whereabouts to her as soon as she stops avoiding me and gives me the time to have an honest conversation. I was hoping to talk with her this weekend, but then she decided to attend the bridal show in Biloxi and ended up heading there earlier than expected. Now with what's happened to Sunny, I'm not sure this weekend is the best time."

Mike leans in, and whispers, "Let me give you a little advice, old buddy. This hospital waiting room is not the place for you and Kristen to get into it. I don't know what her state of mind is going to be like when she arrives, but you need to keep her calm, even if that means walking away or leaving. Besides the fact that it's not an appropriate place to have the type of conversation you'll be having. There will also be watchful eyes and listening ears. Eyes looking for answers, and ears seeking details to gossip about. With the magnitude of Sunny's injuries, people will be searching for details to put a story together about what happened. You don't want to end up on social media or even worse."

"Well, James," Misty adds, "there're sure to be questions about what happened to Sunny, especially how you ended up in the ambulance with her." She gets up to make a complimentary cup of coffee from the hospital-provided pot when a doctor appears with an update. Sunny has been taken into surgery to repair her broken jaw, which will be wired shut for a few weeks. She also suffered broken ribs, and her broken nose will be straightened and set. They are still checking for organ damage and possible internal bleeding. The doctor warns us that Sunny will have stitches in her face and extensive bruising and that a member of his team will provide an update after the surgery concludes, which will take a couple of hours. It's bad, but it could have been even worse, he reports, if she hadn't been found before the bleeding turned extensive. With that news, Mike and I converse at the coffeepot, relieved that Sunny is hanging on, before returning to sit on each end of Chloe, who is now fast asleep on a couch, while Misty steps away on a phone call. The fact that she puts a great distance between her and us indicates that she's probably talking to Kristen and doesn't want me to overhear.

"Well, James," starts Mike, "I don't guess we'll be going to Tiger Land for the game tomorrow." He strongly pats me on the shoulder.

I correct him, "You mean *today*. It's already two o'clock in the morning." Attention turns to the television for a breaking news story reporting a "brutal assault and potential rape" occurring at a local hotel, which was the result of a bachelor party turned bad. Allegedly overindulgence in alcohol is to blame for the crime, and the suspects escaped from the hotel on foot; however, their images were captured on video footage from neighboring businesses. The assailants' identities have not yet been obtained, but the information should be revealed shortly. As a secondary note, the reporter, still live at the scene, continues to share that extensive damage was left in the hotel room where the incident happened, and she is interviewing guests down the hall while hotel security attempts to guide patrons back into their respective rooms. Just then Kristen arrives at the hospital and is intercepted by Misty; they must have been communicating the entire time and devised a plan for Kristen not to face me alone. Apparently Kristen couldn't seem to return my call on her long drive, but she surely made the time to talk with Misty. I'm not surprised.

Kristen and Misty huddle near the entryway doors that occasionally slide open to accommodate new patients, and they seem unfazed. She has yet to acknowledge my presence. Now and then I catch a few words of their conversation as it travels through the corridor. Kristen is chatting at a speedy pace, and I pick up the words *Mom, Drew, sister, lies, fake,* and *confront.* While a few of those terms may be fitting to describe Kristen's feelings toward me, the words *Mom, sister,* and *Drew* certainly do not. *What are they talking about, and why isn't the conversation about what just happened to Sunny?*

From my peripheral vision, I see the pair finally make their way toward Mike and me. I stand up to embrace Kristen, and she returns an icy friendship-style hug, never making eye contact with me. I know that when Kristen gets emotionally stressed, she tends to fidget. Only wanting to comfort her, I instinctively reach for her hand, and she lets me hold it momentarily. I sense her uneasiness because she's a terrible actress, so I play it off by offering to get the girls some coffee, and Mike joins me in the quest while Chloe continues in silent slumber.

***

Misty begins. "I'm waiting for the doors to fly open any minute with police officers coming to question James. Like I told you on the phone, Sunny saw him at that hotel room, and he's the one who rode over in the ambulance with her."

"Do you think James had anything to do with the beating?" Kristen starts crying. "I've never known him to be physical that way, but what if he knew that Sunny had seen him and was worried that she would tell me he was with that woman in a hotel room? Sunny had no idea that I already knew James was going there. I wish she would have fled that scene when she noticed James or as soon as you got off the phone with her. Hell, I *really* wish she would have confronted him herself. At least she wouldn't be in surgery right now."

"Kristen, you know James better than anybody. Do you think he would do something like this to protect himself? That doesn't seem in line with James's character. He's always been the nice guy, the kind that helps little old grannies cross the street."

"I know, I know. I've just seen a very different side of him lately—not abusive in any way, but not the same person I've spent most of my life with. People change. If he's involved in this in any way, first, I'd never forgive him for what he did to Sunny. Second, it would destroy our whole lives. Both of our businesses would be ruined, our reputations publicly shattered, and our marriage officially terminated. I have to believe that the reason for him 'finding Sunny in that condition' is truly that he was meant to be in that place at that time to save her life. Now the reason he was there in the first place is another sad story, for me at least."

"The guys are walking back this way. Take a deep breath and hold it together. If it helps, just think about what Sunny is going through right now. Keep the focus on her. Try to avoid interrogating James right now. You'll have plenty of time to get an extension to the answers you already know. By the way, did I tell you that her jaw is cracked and will be wired shut? She, more than James, is going to need our strength."

Chapter 12

Directly from the hospital at 7:00 a.m. with the news that Sunny's surgery was successful and that she would be unconscious in the ICU for several more hours, I head straight to Formal Affairs to catch up on some work, review the appointment schedule for the next few days, and simply process the last few days' events privately. Luckily I had overpacked for the bridal show and still have several outfits from which to choose, although all are too dressy to sport sitting by myself in the shop. I don't care. I'm happy to not have to go home for now and face James.

I shower at the store and consider my wardrobe options. Today I intend to confront Mary Ann about Drew's shocking news that we are siblings, and I need a power color to pull this off. Considering the disaster of the red dress, I opt for a royal-blue pantsuit. My current state of mind leaves me ill-prepared, offering not a shred of confidence that the color red demands. I had called Mother to request a meeting—yes, there are a number of formalities that exist, even between this mother-and-daughter pair. She makes it a point to brag about her full calendar and goes on and on about her admirers and how in demand her presence is in social circles. Unfortunately, or maybe *fortunately*, the call went unanswered, and a voice message was left. I plan to be here all day, so I asked if she could stop by on her way back from the bridal bizarre.

The store will be especially quiet today because it's Sunday. There won't be any brides-to-be searching for the perfect dress to marry the man of their dreams. No women in denial over their numeric true sizes trying to squeeze into dresses crafted for preteens who have yet to develop curves and busts. Occasionally Misty and I meet here on Sunday to review the status of gown and tuxedo arrivals and order new sample bridesmaid gowns, but Misty won't be coming in today. She's waiting at the hospital. We've agreed to alternate so that Sunny will never be alone. She has no one, and we can't let her wake up in the state she's in not knowing where she is or what happened to her. Poor Sunny is in for a long recovery.

I've always found comfort in solitude. I've never had to be entertained, and I appreciated the rare times to think without interruption, times to contemplate my thoughts and reset my mind to a place of soundness. Being levelheaded and responsible are strong suits of mine, and I always decide on a common-sense approach to problem-solving. It's the very reason I've habitually been labeled the designated driver and why friends have often sought my advice. I'm rolling through my thoughts, reflecting on the most recent past and the actions leading up to the inevitable demise of my marriage, wondering when the path turned so bumpy and what actions of mine contributed to it.

Tap, tap, tap. There's a series of gentle knocks on the beveled glass door. *I can't seem to get one fucking hour to myself!* Fixing my suit and approaching the door with the sign that clearly reads, "Closed," I detect Dreamy Chad on the outside. *What is he doing here on a Sunday?*

"Hey, Kristen, I'm so glad you're here today. I didn't expect anyone to be here on a Sunday. My truck is loaded down with boxes for you, and I wouldn't feel comfortable leaving them on the porch with the rain coming. It's our lucky day!"

"Oh great, Chad!" I say happily. "We've been waiting for a few orders that have been delayed, and you are saving me from having to face some angry bridezillas tomorrow! You're a lifesaver!"

Chad proceeds to unload the truck, placing boxes in our storage area for me to sort through later. I offered to help him, but he insisted that I simply hold the door open for him to pass through. This works for me. When he finishes unloading, he comes in so that I can sign the delivery confirmation. I offer him a soft drink and ask him to sit down. I don't mind his company.

He says, "I'll cool off for a few minutes if you don't mind, and then I'll be out of your way."

"Chad, I'm actually glad you stopped in today. I have to tell you something that happened overnight." I can tell he senses the seriousness in my tone and expression and looks unnerved.

"What happened?" he asks. "Are you OK?"

"It's not me; it's Sunny. She's in the hospital in the ICU. She was assaulted last night at the hotel where she was attending a bachelor party. She went through surgery a few hours ago. She has broken ribs, a broken nose, black eyes, and her jaw is wired shut. She's still being monitored for internal bleeding. I don't know yet if her teeth were affected, but, Chad, she's in a bad way. If James hadn't found her, who knows what the outcome would have been." Chad sits back on the velvet, plush couch, shaking his head from left to right in disbelief. He sits there, apparently processing the devasting news he was just hit with. When he's finally ready to verbalize his thoughts, his disbelief readily morphs into anger.

"How could this happen? Why was Sunny at a bachelor party anyway? That's no place for a single woman to be.

If she wanted to date this guy, she…no, *HE* should have insisted it they meet somewhere else, somewhere safe for a young woman to be! I don't know who this guy is, but I already don't like him. He seems sleazy for suggesting that stupid idea. And look at the result; Sunny's lying in a hospital bed, beaten and broken! I know Sunny's no angel, but she didn't deserve this to happen. Whatever happened to the notion of treating a woman like a lady rather than a conquest or a piece of ass!"

Wow, Chad's really *passionate about this; maybe he has some unexplored feelings for Sunny. Maybe when she's fully recovered, either Misty or I can approach this topic with him. We would love for Sunny to come into good fortune and finally settle down, especially with a decent man like Chad.*

"Did this *mystery date* do this to her? Or was it a group assault? Do the police have any leads?" Before I can answer, he halts his questioning as if struck with a revelation. "Wait a minute, Kristen, what was *James* doing there, at a hotel?"

Now it's my turn to feel deflated. Looking directly at Chad, he senses my hesitation in speaking, and he immediately knows where this conversation is going. A place of hurt and humiliation for me. A hurt that I haven't been ready to openly share.

"I'm so sorry, Kristen. I should keep my big mouth shut. I was out of line, and I never meant to make you uncomfortable. It's none of my business. Please erase that question from your mind."

His overapologetic manner is a bit much, or is it? *Could Chad really be this "dreamy," just a downright genuine, respectful man? There's something about you, Chad, that puts me at ease and knocks down my defenses.*

"It's fine, Chad, don't give it another thought. I'm not one for freely sharing my business with the public, but I'm also not naïve either. I'm well aware that anyone who pays the tiniest bit of attention could detect there's trouble in paradise for me and James." Starting to feel comfortable that I'm in confidential company, the mound of pressure I've been holding on my shoulders begins to crumble and flow freely. Relief is in sight, and there's no turning back now. Chad tunes in attentively and makes no movement as I take a seat next to him on the couch. Our eyes lock, and the stare is held infinitely.

"You know, Chad, James and I have been together for an eternity, ever since high school anyway. We grew into adulthood together and each knew undoubtedly that our futures contained each other. Whether it was simple innocence, childish inexperience talking, or plain stupidity, I pictured life going in one direction, with all roads traveled with James. But life has its challenges. People grow and change their minds, and sometimes the hand you're dealt isn't the one you were expecting." Chad nods knowingly.

This is my cue to proceed. "Throughout all the years we've been together, I never had a doubt about James's commitment to me and our marriage. Again it may be that I've been too trusting when I shouldn't have been. Or perhaps signs existed along the way and I chose avoidance. If you don't acknowledge it, it didn't happen, right? I believe they call it 'turning a blind eye.' Either way I'm done"—I flick my hand carelessly in the air—"with foolish thoughts of unwavering commitment. Chad, James has been cheating on me."

"Hold on, Kristen," Chad interjects. "Are you sure you're OK sharing your personal information with me? I wouldn't want you ever to regret confiding in me. Our friendship means too much to me." Again Chad seems genuine with those caring eyes, as he scoots the slightest bit closer to me on the couch. The sincerity in his words surfaces from a place of thoughtful concern—something I haven't experienced in quite some time.

"It's fine, Chad. I've held everything in—"

He interrupts, "You mean outside of Misty, of course?" He snickers and so do I. It feels good. His awareness of the closeness of my and Misty's relationship reveals another layer of Chad's intuitiveness.

"Look, I have proof. I've seen it for myself, so there's no doubt in my mind. Please don't ask me to suffer through the details again. Just believe me when I say that my marriage has entered the point of no return. Expect to hear that bit of gossip, although it will be factual, as you deliver packages all over town." With that, Chad leans in and gently wipes the tear from the corner of my eye.

"Don't worry, Kristen, I won't spread gossip about you and James. Friends protect each other, and I will shut down any negative comments I come across. I hope you know that I am here for you to talk to at any time. You're not alone. I told you before that I'll always be here for you. I meant it then, and I completely mean it now. I promise you, Kristen, you won't be alone. Well, I guess I better get going for now." Chad stands to leave, and I join him.

"Wait, Chad." In an instant, I go in for a kiss, and it is not only accepted but returned. Delicate at first, but then building from gentle to intense. I feel the heat of released emotion, of raw physical expression with a trusted partner. Pent-up desire is given freely to an eager lover. Roaming hands happily reciprocate my animalistic grasps as we enter cycles of penetrating pleasure. And so it spontaneously happens. Formal Affairs witnesses my unplanned revenge sex with Dreamy Chad.

Chapter 13

Rain beats heavily down on Formal Affairs this afternoon, providing me with ample reflection time back in my somewhat-wrinkled blue suit. One never considers the feelings experienced post-extramarital naughty sex prior to doing it. I didn't know what to expect. If asked in the past, I probably would have described the emotions with adjectives like ashamed, embarrassed, regretful, or even mortified. From the vantage point of experience, I can now answer the question.

I feel none of those emotions. I resemble an ice cube with a cold, hard exterior slowly melting into cool flowing water, yet also like a sheet of crisp computer paper, plain and unmarked with nothing to share. I can't say that I feel happy or sad about what transpired between me and Chad just a few hours ago because I honestly don't feel responsive about any of it. Putting things into perspective, I found solace in the company of a friend that irresponsibly turned physical. It's not supposed to happen that way. And while I frequently joked with Misty about having revenge sex and even coming close with Antonio in Biloxi, I could never initiate or partake. Mother's crap about purity and lessons in prudence overshadowed any potential contradictory actions. Subconsciously, I must have been trying to punish James, to make him hurt as I hurt. Maybe he'll never find out, and my spiteful point will not even be inflicted. In such a case, how sweet is revenge really? Glaring out the window, headlights shine back at me. The South has known no storm like the one coming to Formal Affairs. It's Hurricane Mary Ann.

In her usual manner, she blows in with force. Is her hair messed up? Of course not, even in this treacherous thunderstorm. She has it wrapped in a plastic covering tied under her chin because heaven forbid she is caught unkempt in public. Scanning me from top to bottom, she takes in my stunning blue suit and patent-leather pumps. With a raised eyebrow, she inquisitively notes, "A wee bit dressed up to be sitting all alone on a Sunday, aren't you, Kristen?"

I can always count on you to exercise your right to cast judgment.

"I heard the terrible news this morning about your employee being attacked last night. How awful, although I should have come across this information from *you*, my daughter, rather than receiving it secondhand, but I'll skip right over that for now. If you ask me, Sunny was asking for trouble. I've seen the way she throws herself at the men in this very store. Very unladylike. What did she expect to happen when she taunts men, shamelessly flirting with them to the point of embarrassment and degradation? You can't play such dangerous games with the opposite sex! I suppose if she had received a decent upbringing, she would have known better."

"Enough! I've heard enough! You know nothing about Sunny and her upbringing or lack thereof. She's a very nice person and a stellar employee; she's like family to me and Misty." Mary Ann purses her lips tightly together with a disapproving expression on her flawlessly painted face for my outburst. "Sunny was a victim of a violent crime last night, and she is still in the ICU. She didn't ask for this to happen to her. We're only hoping she'll recover fully and return to work because everyone here will miss her presence. She's a positive influence and never speaks poorly about anyone. I'm glad you mentioned the word *upbringing*, though. I asked you to meet with me today because I have a few questions about my upbringing and yours."

"Whatever are you talking about, Kristen?" Mom wearily responds. "I brought you up the same way I was brought up, with modesty and pristine moral standards."

"Could you please expand on that? What exactly do you mean by *modesty* and *pristine moral standards*? I may need some clarity."

"Sure, dear. For starters, young ladies exercising modesty properly cover themselves throughout all seasons so as not to dress in a revealing manner. They take pride in their conservative appearances. As for morals, young ladies further behave in such a way as to demonstrate pride for themselves as they adhere to high standards for females. They exude femininity. They do not find themselves in compromising positions that could tarnish their personal reputations or the reputation of their families. Does that clear things up for you?"

"Only partially. I understand the definition of the terms, but I wanted to know if this is how *you've* always lived. I mean, I remember the teachings about being a good girl and saving sex for marriage, but is this how you've lived, Mother?"

She stands more upright, looks me dead in the eye, and proceeds to spew untruth. "Of course I have! I don't know what the real meaning of this conversation is, Kristen, but I can assure you these are tenants by which I have led my life and instilled the importance of proper behavior in you, young lady. They represent the possession of utmost character and pride. I have always carried myself like the lady I am and have encouraged nothing short of that behavior from you as well! Because of my prudent demeanor, I am recognized and lead numerous social clubs, remember? I radiate virtuosity and stand for nothing less from my acquaintances. As we *are* judged by the company we keep, I would not allow anyone or anything to diminish my noble stature in this community."

Having had my fill of the bullshit, I blurt out, "How about a son?"

She immediately snaps to attention. "What did you say? You're speaking foolishly. I don't have a son."

"Oh, Mother, but you do. And I met him. His name is Drew." Suddenly her colorful facial canvas turns pale white, and she's stunned in place. "As I see you're at a loss for words, have a seat while I share some details that may just happen to 'diminish your noble stature.' You see for several weeks now, a man named Drew has been trying to contact me. He left several phone messages and even stopped by, but I wasn't in the office at the time. When we finally connected by phone, which was on my drive to Biloxi Thursday, he asked to meet. I initially thought he was a formalwear vendor, but that was not the case. He wanted to talk about a possible family connection." Mother listens, concentrating on my every word. "At that point, I thought he was looking for a job with Dad. Anyway, he seemed nice enough on the phone, so I agreed to meet him Friday morning before the bridal bizarre started.

Actually you saw him. He was the gentleman you accusingly inferred that I was meeting out of town without my husband's presence. Ring a bell?"

Mary Ann wordlessly nods her head in agreement.

"Drew began telling me that he had taken a genetic test, the kind where you send in saliva and register on their database, resulting in family tree connections. Since I had done this myself, my information was there, and it connected us as siblings."

"Well, I've never done anything like that, so it must be a mistake. Or maybe it's the result of one of your father's indiscretions. Either way it's simply not true, Kristen."

"With the evidence that was presented to me, I am going to ask you to stop lying. It's time to face the truth. Drew shared his results with me. I saw firsthand the family tree connection, and it is one hundred percent accurate that he is my brother. Furthermore our connection is on the *maternal* side, not Dad's side. You have a son. I have a brother. What happened? I need you to tell me the truth, and the old 'I think I'm going to faint' act is not going to work this time."

Confronted with facts and backed into a corner, Mary Ann is ready to release secrets of her own. That is once I hand her a fresh cup of coffee and the tissue she is motioning for.

"Kristen, I have worked my entire adult life to make up for an accident that occurred when I was just a young girl. I tried to be a perfect mother for you, teaching you the rights and wrongs of society so that you could enjoy your life guilt free, unlike me. When I was seventeen years old, I fell in love with a dashing young man who basically took my breath away. He had recently graduated from high school, and that summer before he was to leave for college we lived. I mean, we were determined to fit everything into those few months. We knew we had limited time left together, and we made every second count. Although I tried to convince him to stay in town, his family wouldn't hear of it. They, and he, had big plans for his future success. He was to earn a business degree and support his family's developing construction business, agreeing to return home to run the company if they paid the college tuition. We found time and places to be alone together, and I gave in to our physical connection on more than one occasion. I knew it was wrong, but I was desperate to share everything with him. My inexperience led me to believe that once we shared our bodies, we would forever belong to each other. That he wouldn't become involved with other girls out of respect for me and my honor. How foolish of me. Two weeks after he left for college, your grandmother took me to the doctor to treat what my parents believed was food poisoning since I was routinely weak and vomiting. There we shockingly found out that I was pregnant and had to face your grandfather with this news. His initial reaction was sheer anger and disappointment, demanded that a marriage be scheduled. However, after a couple of days to process the situation and to avoid family embarrassment, he and my mother decided it was time for me to 'help a sick aunt' in another state for a few months. I would give birth to my baby there and return home when 'Aunt Sue recovered from her illness.' As a minor I had no rights and no other options. They made all the arrangements and signed papers. I was forced to put my child up for adoption. The baby was taken before I could see it. I was never told if it was a boy or a girl. I suppose it was better that way, but all these years I had no idea what became of my child." Tears flowed freely from my mother's sad eyes. She took a deep breath and continued.

"I had told the father that I would wait for him to come back from college, and we could raise our child together, but he said no because his family would never approve. At that time bringing a child into the world that was conceived out of wedlock was a disgrace to a family, and I would be deemed a whore. I pleaded with him to marry me, and everything would work out, but the societal pressure was too much for him to bear. He knew that it would be uncovered that I was already pregnant, especially with the idea of a shotgun wedding, and the charade would be revealed. He would be disowned and broke, and that was a gamble he was not willing to take. Neither suggestion was possible back then. It was a different time."

"Wow, this is incredible, Mom. It's incredible that I have a brother. It's incredible that you will have your questions answered. And it's incredible that you kept this secret for so long. How did you manage to do that?" I sincerely sympathize with her story and the strength she had endured all those years ago. A single girl shipped off to avoid bringing shame to the family.

"Well, Kristen, in the spirit of full disclosure, it's not a secret."

Wait, what?

"Our community was not that big, and I knew I would cross paths with the father again because our families were close friends. When he returned from college, he was engaged to someone. I knew our time together had expired, but I felt he deserved to know what happened. Together we, with his fiancé, spent months searching for an infant born during that time but were unsuccessful. We've remained close ever since and jointly hoped that one day we would discover what we yearned to find. As for your father, I told him the whole story when he proposed to me. I felt he deserved to know, even though he would have been within his rights to desert me, as society would have deemed me *damaged goods* back then. He stood by me, and that's why I've also stood by him, considering his own imperfections and infidelity." She gives me a wink.

"But, Mother, you said you remained close with the father of your child and his fiancé. Do I know who they are?"

"Yes, my dear Kristen. You know them very well and so does James. It's Henry and Rose."

Chapter 14

Why did I agree to meet James today? He couldn't have chosen a worse time. I need space to internalize what happened with Chad. I'm having a hard time processing what happened, and I don't know that I am emotionally ready to be slapped in the face with his infidelities. Why do I have to anyway? He obviously doesn't want to be married to me anymore; I've had my revenge sex, so I don't feel like such a pathetic victim, so let's go to divorce court and move on with our respective lives.

I'm pulling up at the house, and surprisingly my heart isn't even beating fast. I guess I know that the end is near, and I am ready to put an end to all the deception. The door is unlocked, and music is playing in the background. How fitting, it's Luke Bryan's "Do I," a song about a partner wondering if they still "turn on" their lover. I can easily provide the answer to that question with little effort. I approach and enter the bedroom and happen upon James sitting on the bed and staring at the TV. He looks stone-faced and mad as hell.

"Did you...*sleep* with him, Kristen?" He can barely speak the words.

"What?" I ask, shocked that he is scrolling through my cell phone.

"Don't lie to me. Did you sleep with Chad?" He demands an answer. I'm caught off guard by this instant interrogation. He looks up at me with unfamiliar rage in his bloodshot eyes. "I saw you. I saw you and Chad kissing. Stupid me, thinking I could pop in and actually catch you alone so that we could have a long overdue conversation. Only you were NOT alone, Kristen! You were wrapped up in another man's arms, kissing him! I can't fucking believe this! How could you do this to me, to us?

"Surprise, surprise! Yeah, James, I did. Just like you. You don't think I know you've been doing the same thing?" I lash out. "Yep, I let Chad touch me and have sex with me, just the way you've been doing it. Now *you* get to experience the hurt and betrayal I've felt for months!" He looks at me with disbelief and confusion. "What's the matter, a case of amnesia setting in? Well let me refresh your memory about the redheaded slut you've been texting and meeting up with?" His posture tenses up, and his face reddens

153

as he rises to his feet and begins nervously pacing back and forth. "You didn't think I knew, did you? Oh, ever so smart James, planning secret meetings at our Coffee & Cocktails—OUR place! Sending secret text messages when I'm in the shower! Meeting her in a hotel room!" *Boy, am I letting him have it! The great reveal!*

"Oh my God, oh my God, Kristen. What have you done? What have you fucking done? I have been meeting with a redhead behind your back." Dropped to the ground, hands pulling at his own hair in turmoil, he's suddenly crying.

Something doesn't seem right. This isn't the scene of an adulterer being caught and confronted. Dare I ask him what's with this reaction? I stand silent for a minute.

"Open the fucking desk drawer!" he yells. Not sure what to expect, I oblige his request and see an unmarked white leather portfolio.

"I really don't need you to share the details of your sordid sexual tryst, James. I've seen and heard enough on my own for months!"

That comment hits just the right nerve, and James jumps up from the floor, rips the folder from my shaking hands, and violently shakes it, emptying its contents onto the floor. He flings the empty folder, propelling it across the room before it hits the glass lamp, knocking it over and shattering it into pieces.

"Stop it, you're scaring me!" He's unresponsive to my command. "What is all of this, James, divorce papers? You could have me served another way instead of throwing them all over the house!"

"No, Kristen, my unfaithful wife, it's not divorce papers!" Flipping them over, he reveals what looks like blueprints. "It's your fucking house, Kristen! The house you and I talked about and planned for years now. This was the house you always wanted. No picket fence!"

"I don't understand." My eyes are filling with tears, and breathing becomes burdensome. "What house? What does this have to do with you cheating on me?"

"The redhead is Cassidy Laine, Rose and Henry's niece. She is an in-demand architect, and I've been meeting up secretly with her to have your dream house designed as a surprise for our tenth anniversary. That's it. Nothing more and Rose has been covering for me whenever you called so I could steal some time to view the drafts. I swore her to secrecy."

"But I saw the two of you myself in Corks & Cocktails. You were pretty chummy and visibly flirting. I saw you sitting side-by-side and even watched you order a bourbon!"

"We were sitting next to each other because she was showing me her ideas for the house, some of her previous work, and the cutting-edge designs she thought you might like. And yes I ordered a fucking bourbon! I was proud and wanted to celebrate the fact that I could finally build my wife the home she had always wanted."

Chapter 15

Everything is different today. This special day marks a significant turning point for me, having come full circle and inspired to experience life anew.

I stare out the window of Mia's Italian Eatery, the place James texted to suggest we meet for lunch. I'm the first to arrive, so I quickly secure the best table for people-watching, centered on the expansive glass window. It's the perfect spot to finalize a few thoughts, recording them in my journal to capture their essence in real time while I await James's arrival. Lazily peering at the purple canopy entry to Coffee & Cocktails across the street, I reminisce about happy times crossing into and out of that entryway. The countless celebrations—whether birthdays, anniversaries, meeting old friends, or simply popping in to connect with coworkers over drinks—that place holds so many of my precious memories. I catch James's outline on the sidewalk through that same glass as he approaches Mia's and know deep down in my heart that both places, along with those treasured memories, belong to him too. As he approaches the table ever so gently, I ease the precious journal into my awaiting bag. *I'll visit with you again in a little bit.*

"Sorry, I'm a little late," he apologizes, and kisses me on the head. "Since we're heading to the beach for our anniversary trip, I had to return a few calls. I want our time together to be uninterrupted, free from work." He scans me up and down with approving eyes and compliments my outfit, raises his eyebrows, smiles mischievously, and states, "I obviously remember the last time you wore it. I vividly remember that it was the last time we met up at Pat's Bar, pretending to be strangers, flirting shamelessly before enjoying a happy ending. You really need to wear it more often. The way that camel-colored suede miniskirt hugs those hips so tightly and sexy thigh-high stiletto boots has my dick hard already. You know I'm a goner when you wear that animal-print blouse that shows me just a bit of those luscious breasts, baby. Are you trying to torture me in public? If I stand, the whole damn place will spot the bulge and see what you do to me."

The waitress approaches with a tray holding the drinks I preordered, anticipating James's impending arrival. It's his usual drink of choice, Crown and Coke, a whiskey man through and through, and a delicate glass of red wine for me. "Thanks for the drink, babe. Have I told you lately how gorgeous you are and that I can't imagine loving you more than I do right now?" I love it when James flirts with me.

I smile bashfully. "Oh, silly old me?"

James comments that he noticed I made it to my hair appointment this morning. "Your hair looks great. It's shiny too."

I reply that I colored my hair to incorporate red highlights, teasing him that tonight he could try sleeping with a redhead. He laughs and teasingly asks exactly which name is assigned to the man I would like him to imitate in the bedroom tonight. "How about Antonio? It's fitting since we love Italian so much! See if you can perfect a sexy Italian accent to accompany your new identity," I say in a seductive voice.

James's phone rings, and noticing the name on the screen, he shares, "It's Mike," as he hits the button to take the call. "Go ahead and order for me while I talk to Mike."

"I already have while I was waiting for you to get here. It's all good; take care of business because once we leave here, we are going totally unplugged, you got that?" His wink and million-dollar grin shows he readily accepts the conditions.

The waitress approaches with the meals, placing the heavy ceramic plates on the table. "Yum, it's my favorite

159

savory meatballs. I hope you'll still want to kiss me later with my garlic breath," he admits.

"Kissing is only the beginning, my super sexy husband. I have more in store for you," I reply.

"Hold that thought, sweetheart, nature calls. I'll be back in a minute." James motions to the waitress, who is scrolling through her phone, to request a second round of drinks before retreating to the restroom while I pull out my journal again.

Briefly alone for the final time on my journey of exploration and reflection, I'm so happy to be writing my final chapter. I relish a few secluded, final moments to dwell in my fictional realities created this past year, the charting of consequential chance events—my dreams, my serendipity. The occupants of my mind's eye—scenarios of adultery, threatened friendships, private conversations, secrets, and betrayal of the worst kind, infidelity. If only in my mind, I profoundly consider potential fallouts of negligent behavior, such as reckless flirtations and the hurt left when irresponsibility impacts and potentially threatens life. Discovering I have a brother, a true event, nonetheless, was a fact hidden from me my entire life because Mother would never accept her own indiscretions and humanity when she, herself, failed to be a "good girl."

Scenarios resulting in various potential consequences monopolized my imagination and consumed my thoughts for long enough. Fantasizing about being a naughty girl has done wonders for my sex life and my marriage in general. Through creativity and a little research, I have become emboldened to give freely of my body, unworried about societal stereotypes. Through storytelling, I've mapped out possible outcomes, penalty-filled, of behaving like a promiscuous being from a safe zone—my imagination. I've been able to feel the magnitude of projected heartbreak from afar. I know without a doubt, more now than I ever believed possible, that I could never cheat on James, my one true love, my soulmate, my everything. I could never jeopardize the love we've nurtured from mere teenagers, and I will fight mightily to preserve what we have... what's mine. I am ready to give up the self-inflicted condemnation for thinking dirty thoughts and exploring my own sexuality from the safety of my own marital bed. I am emerging as a self-confident, liberated woman without regret or apology with no one to impress but myself and my husband.

Alas, I examine the weathered navy journal's cover, embossed with my initials, KNM, one last time before putting the invented tales to rest. I gently run my fingers over the feel of the worn leather, circling the monogram. This journal has been my lifeline, exposing my insecurities and testing the waters of someone else's experiences, although by dreams and conjuring. Oddly it has become my security, my treasured confidant, but this dependency, too, has served its purpose.

I hug my journal one last time before gently and reluctantly surrendering it into the bag, and the action tugs at my heart. James is returning to the table, his cocky smile so full of promise. Some still may believe that mother knows best. That notion is truly debatable and certainly situational. As for me there's no guilt to bear for being a *good* girl.

Milton Keynes UK
Ingram Content Group UK Ltd.
UKHW021422231024
450026UK00012BA/776